TROUBLE WITH Will

MYLA JACKSON

ELLORA'S CAVE
ROMANTICA PUBLISHING

What the critics are saying...

ଚ୬

5 Flags "In conjunction with laugh-out-loud humor are explosive love scenes that will leave you begging for more!"

~ *Euroreviews*

"For a light-hearted and thoroughly enjoyable erotic adventure, pick up a copy of Myla Jackson's TROUBLE WITH WILL today." ~ *Romance Reviews Today*

An Ellora's Cave Romantica Publication

www.ellorascave.com

Trouble with Will

ISBN 9781419956669
ALL RIGHTS RESERVED.
Trouble with Will Copyright © 2006 Myla Jackson
Edited by Briana St. James
Cover art by Willo

This book is printed in the U.S.A. by Jasmine–Jade Enterprises, LLC.

Electronic book Publication June 2006
Trade paperback Publication June 2007

Excerpt from *Ghost Wind* Copyright © Charlotte Boyett-Compo, 2007

Also by Myla Jackson

ଛ

Ellora's Cavemen: Dreams of the Oasis I (*anthology*)
Jacq's Warlord *wirh Delilah Devlin*
Sex, Lies & Vampire Hunters
Shewolf
Trouble with Harry
Witch's Curse

About the Author

ଛ

I've written for Ellora's Cave since September of 2006 when my first release Trouble with Harry came out. Since then, I've expanded from reluctant genies to werewolves, chameleons, vampires and witches. For me, reading and writing gives me the freedom to explore strange new worlds and write the characters and creatures clamoring to escape my mind. I like writing everything from romantic comedy to dark and sexy suspense. Mostly I like to escape into other worlds whether grounded in reality or complete fantasy. Come…escape with me!

Myla welcomes comments from readers. You can find her website and email address on her author bio page at www.ellorascave.com.

Tell Us What You Think
We appreciate hearing reader opinions about our books. You can email us at Comments@EllorasCave.com.

TROUBLE WITH WILL

❦

Trademarks Acknowledgement

ഇൻ

The author acknowledges the trademarked status and trademark owners of the following wordmarks mentioned in this work of fiction:

AK-47: Cold Steel, Inc.

Google: Google Inc.

Indiana Jones: Lucasfilm Ltd.

Ringling Brothers Barnum & Bailey Circus: Ringling Bros.–Barnum & Bailey Combined Shows, Inc.

Chapter One
Riyadh, Saudi Arabia

ഇ

Kate Ralston slipped through the dingy streets of the grittier area of Riyadh. Draped in a black *abaya* with the *hijab* veil pulled up around her face hiding all but her eyes, she blended in with the Arabic women hurrying to and from the open-air markets. She looked like any other Saudi female unless someone looked close enough to see her eyes weren't the normal deep brown of women of Arabic descent. Kate's were an icy blue. She kept her head down and followed her guide moving quietly through the maze of narrow alleys and crowded streets until they reached a dark doorway in an even darker passage between a pair of four-story buildings.

Her guide knocked twice and, before Kate could stop him, he disappeared back the way they'd come. Good riddance. He'd smelled like a rancid camel. Fortunately he'd done his job and gotten her to her rendezvous. Along the way Kate had paid close attention, fairly confident she could find her way back to her hotel in the more affluent section of the city.

A prickle of awareness slithered across her skin and she shot a glance over her shoulder. People passed on the busy street they'd turned off but no one ventured into the alley. Still, she had that unnerving sensation of being watched. She hoped the hell her American contact, Todd Jones, hadn't set her up as a candidate for the white slave trade. He'd seemed the slippery sort, but he was the only person with any information on the Eye of the Serpent.

The door opened in front of her and she was jerked inside. When an arm clamped around her throat, she dropped into a crouch and threw her elbow into her attacker's gut.

He gasped, doubling over.

Kate slipped beneath his arm, snapping it up behind him and between his shoulder blades. Her heart pounding in her chest, she held firm with one hand. With the other, she pushed the hood from her head and then yanked the *hijab* off her face. There, now she could see and breathe. How did women put up with all the layers?

The man struggled to free himself. "Lighten up, lady! You're gonna break my fuckin' arm!" Kate recognized the nasal voice as Todd's, a wheeler-dealer and all-around sleazebag of the Arab world.

"Next time, I will. Don't fuck with me, Toad." She ratcheted the arm farther up his back before she let it go.

"The name's Todd." He stepped out of her reach and shook his wrist, glaring at her. "I've a good mind to tell Sabirah the deal's off."

"You won't if you value your life." Kate hadn't come this far for Toad-the-Sleaze to get cold feet. She pulled the knife from her arm strap and held it beneath Todd's chin. "Now, show me the Eye of the Serpent before I slit your throat."

"God, I hate pushy broads."

"There's something you ought to know about me." She nicked his throat with the tip of her knife and a drop of blood oozed down his neck. "I don't like it when guys call me a broad."

Sweat beaded on Todd's brow. "Okay, okay. Keep your shirt on."

"Absolutely." She stepped away and sheathed the knife in the sleeve of the *abaya*, glad for the voluminous folds and the handy things she could hide in their depths. Her eyes adjusting to the dim lighting, she made note of the bright orange and red cushions strewn around the room. An intricately woven Persian carpet covered the floor indicating more wealth than she expected in this seedier side of the capital of Saudi Arabia. "So where's Sabirah? I don't have all day."

"I am here," a voice said behind her in an articulate English accent.

Kate spun to face a portly, dark-skinned Arab.

Framed by the doorway, he stood draped in white, with a black-and-white *kaffiyeh*, the traditional Arabic headdress, affixed to his head with black braided *Agal*. An impressive figure, but not one that intimidated Kate. Not much did.

With a nod, Kate acknowledged his presence. "Kate Ralston."

His head dipped. "I am Sabirah. I've heard of you, Miss Ralston."

Not one to waste words, Kate got right to the point of her visit. "You have the Eye of the Serpent?"

"I do." Sabirah nodded toward Todd-the-Sleaze.

The younger man moved toward the door, muttering to her as he passed, "Don't screw up this deal, Ralston."

Kate ignored him. Todd had only been a means to this meeting with Sabirah. Now the man was superfluous and the sooner he left the better. The guy made her skin crawl.

Todd slipped out leaving Kate and Sabirah alone in the room.

She'd come for the Eye of the Serpent and nothing would get in her way of that goal.

Sabirah waved a hand toward the cushions. "*Ahlan wa-sahlan.* Welcome. Please, take a seat."

With her instincts screaming for her to get the object and leave quickly, Kate forced herself to sit cross-legged on a cushion.

"You have come a long way to purchase this precious stone." He folded his arms, tucking his hands inside his sleeves. "I have worked with many collectors of fine art and antiquities, but never a collector quite so beautiful and…shall I say, determined?"

Impatience rode strong beneath the surface of her calm as she inhaled and blew out a slow steady breath. "I appreciate the finer things in life."

"And the Eye is a rare piece indeed, but not unknown. Are you familiar with the legend behind the gem?"

Deciding it might be worthwhile to play dumb, Kate shook her head. "No, I'm not."

Sabirah leaned forward, his eyes narrowing like a storyteller preparing to reveal a deep, dark secret. "The Eye of the Serpent is said to be the key to Sand City."

Just the mention of the legendary city made Kate's heart skip. "Sand City?" She shrugged stiff shoulders, aiming for casual and probably falling short. "Never heard of it."

"Oh, surely you jest. Wasn't your father on an expedition in search of the great city when he disappeared into the desert?"

"I only know of his humanitarian assistance to the Bedouins. He never mentioned Sand City." Now she was out-and-out lying and she schooled her face like she did when she played poker. Show no emotion, no fear and no regret. Her father had taught her the art of the game.

Sabirah pressed his fingers together in a steeple and tipped his head back as if assessing the truth of her statement. Finally, he nodded. "Since you expressed an interest in acquiring the Eye of the Serpent, I have received yet another inquiry."

Kate reminded herself not to react, but to remain calm and steady. "May I ask whom?"

"A man claiming to be a friend of yours." Sabirah paused. "Omar Qarim."

Anger rose in Kate's throat and she struggled to keep from spitting it out. She could feel the heat rising in her cheeks and willed it to subside. Men who traded stolen goods, like Sabirah, were known for pitting collectors against each other to demand a higher price. "Ah, Omar. How is my good friend?" The smile was even more difficult than the words, but she strained her lips to curl.

"He is quite anxious to have the Eye of the Serpent." Sabirah sat back and smiled.

"And what did Omar say when you told him the gem was sold?"

"What kind of businessman do you think I am? Of course I did not tell him the gem was sold. I waited for his offer first."

"And?"

Sabirah shook his head. "Much lower than yours, I might say."

Kate sat forward, tired of the game and ready to be gone. "So, where is the Eye?"

"It is not here."

Anger pushed Kate to her feet. "Why you—" For the past year she'd searched for the Eye of the Serpent and this was her only clue, her only lead in all that time—all that time wasted. "If you've lied to me, I swear I'll—"

"Nothing. You will do nothing," he finished for her, patting the mat beside him. "Please, sit. I fully intend to deliver the Eye to you within the hour. It is not safe for you to carry such an object through the streets of Riyadh."

Kate remained standing, her legs slightly apart. "I'll take my chances," she said through gritted teeth. She needed the Eye and she would face a den of terrorists in order to get it.

"As I said, I am in the process of having it delivered to your hotel. You will have the Eye as soon as we complete our transaction." He waved his finger. "There is the matter of payment."

"Why should I pay you now? How do I know you will deliver?" Her hand went to the money belt she wore beneath her *abaya*.

"You will pay me half now and half when the Eye is delivered. Do we have an understanding?"

"And if I don't agree?"

"I'm sure Omar will not have difficulties with the same arrangements and price."

Seething beneath the surface, Kate fought to remain in control of her emotions. What choice did she have? If Omar got hold of the Eye, all would be lost for her father and the people of the Sand City. "Okay. But if I don't get the Eye as promised, I'll kill you. Do we have an understanding?"

Sabirah nodded. "Indeed."

Kate lifted the black *abaya* to her chin, exposing her khaki slacks and black running shoes. She noted the brief flash of disappointment in Sabirah's eyes when he glanced at her clothing. Did he expect her to be naked beneath the *abaya*?

Dumbass. Just because she was an American didn't make her an idiot.

With a flick, she unclipped the money belt from around her waist and dropped it at Sabirah's feet. "Count it. It's all there."

"But isn't that the entire amount?"

"No. I didn't trust you. I only brought half."

Sabirah's cheeks reddened and for a moment and Kate thought he would shout in anger. Instead he laughed out loud. "You are a shrewd dealer. Are you certain you were not born a man?"

"If I had been, I'd have killed you already and taken what I wanted." She gave him a pointed look. "I'll be waiting for the Eye."

"You can expect it in exactly one hour." He snapped his fingers and two young men clad in white robes and

15

white headdresses rushed from the doorway behind him to assist Sabirah to his feet. Once he was standing, he shook their hands loose. "Show this woman to her hotel."

"No thanks. I'll find it on my own." With a final narrow-eyed look at Sabirah, she said, "I want that gem." She hoped he got the underlying subtext to her message. If she didn't get the Eye of the Serpent as promised, Sabirah would be the first to go.

Sabirah nodded. "I understand."

Kate exited, tripping over Todd as she stormed through the opening.

"Ah, I take it your business is concluded satisfact…" His voice faded when she didn't even acknowledge his presence.

Pulling the *hijab* across her face, Kate strode off through the streets intent on returning to her hotel to await delivery of her father's salvation.

When she arrived in her room, hot from the combination of the black *abaya* and the midday heat of the desert sun, she stripped the garment over her head and ducked into the shower to cool off.

As she stepped out of the shower and onto the mat to dry, she heard someone banging on her door. A quick glance at the clock indicated it had only been forty-five minutes. The delivery wasn't supposed to be for another fifteen. Perhaps Sabirah was nervous and sent it earlier than advertised.

Wrapping a large white towel around her middle, she rushed out of the bathroom, her heart skittering in her chest. This was it. Her chance to free her father.

"Just a minute."

She raced to the closet and pulled the rest of the money she owed Sabirah from the tiny room safe and stuffed it between her breasts. Anxious to get her hands on the Eye, she didn't wait to dress. Tucking the towel in tightly over her chest, she whipped open the door.

Two large Arabic men who could be bouncers at a bar stood on the other side, one carrying a plain brown box. Their eyes widened at her state of undress, but they didn't speak. Good. Kate wasn't in the mood to put up with Saudi male chauvinistic bullshit.

"Is this from Sabirah?" she demanded.

The man with the box nodded.

When she reached out to take the box, he swung it away from her. "First the money."

"How do I know my merchandise is inside?"

"You don't. But no money, no box."

This deal smelled worse and worse by the minute. But she had to have the Eye, her father's life depended on it. She dug into her cleavage and brought out the money. "Here. Now let me have the box."

One man took the money, the other shoved the box in her hands and then both walked away.

Kate was already tearing into the tape holding the box together before she even closed the door. When she had the box open her fingers dug into the foam peanuts until they came into contact with a smooth hard object. But it wasn't in the shape of a big round jewel. It had a long neck and fat bottom. She lifted the object from the box and held it up. "Damn you, Sabirah!"

In her hand was an old, blue-green glass bottle covered in a thick layer of dust. It had to be hundreds of years old, maybe thousands. But Kate didn't care. It wasn't the Eye of the Serpent.

Maybe the men hadn't gotten far. Kate dove for the door to her room and stared out. No one stood in the hall. Still clad in her towel, she was in no state to run out into the street chasing them. The Saudi police would have her thrown in jail, stoned or something for running around naked in a country where they didn't see anything but a woman's eyes.

With her stomach knotted and anger boiling in her veins, Kate stormed back into her room and slammed the door. As she passed by her international cell phone on a side table, she grabbed it and punched in the numbers for Toad-the-Sleaze's local cell number.

Damn! Damn! Damn! Sabirah had gotten the best of her and all her money. She'd be double-damned if he got away with it.

"Toad."

"Todd. The name is Todd." He sighed. "What do you want, Kate?"

"You know damn well what I want. And if I don't get it, you and your man Sabirah are dead men," she said.

"What are you talking about?"

"Your delivery men just arrived with the wrong item."

"The Eye of the Serpent was in the box. I made sure myself."

"That's not what made it here. I got some old nasty bottle." She lifted the glass and brushed at the dust with the corner of her towel. "Tell Sabirah I want the Eye of the Serpent or I'll be on him like stink on shit. You got me?"

"I saw the Eye in that box, I swear. Look, Kate, I'll get back to you in two minutes. Let me find out what's happening."

Exactly two minutes later Kate's phone rang.

"Kate, Sabirah swore he sent the Eye of the Serpent," Todd said. "If you didn't get it, it was stolen in transit."

"Damn!" Her fist clenched around the phone. "What about my money?"

"You gave it to the wrong men. Count is as gone. Gotta go, call me if you need anything else. Sorry this didn't work out for you."

"Fuck!" Kate slammed her phone shut and rubbed the towel over the glass again. "Damned ugly bottle, too. I'm going to kill Sabirah if it's the last thing I—what the—"

The floor shook so violently Kate tossed the bottle onto the couch and dropped to her knees. As a rumble of thunder filled the air, she grabbed a cushion from a nearby chair and held it over the back of her neck.

Had there been an earthquake? Did a bomb go off nearby? What the hell was going on?

Then the room went still. Kate eased the cushion aside and ventured a look around.

Her gaze lit on a pair of large bare feet. For a moment she studied the toes until her mind registered these really were feet she was looking at.

She sat up and pushed away as fast as she could. Her heart in her throat, her gaze traveled up ankles, knees and thighs, equally bare to—

"Wow!" Her perusal hung on what was hanging between the thighs. The biggest cock she'd seen on a real man, not one of those pumped-up guys in the porn videos. Dragging her gaze away from his male body parts, she forced herself to find the face that belonged to that incredible — whew!

Heat sizzled along her nerve endings as she looked up a long way to find Adonis staring down at her. No other words could describe his golden-haired, blue-eyed perfection. And he was naked as the day he was born, only fully equipped and quickly becoming fully erect.

Adonis scrubbed a hand down his face. "Where am I?"

For some stupid reason, Kate couldn't find her voice to respond. Myriad questions sifted through her mind, none able to take root. Where had this man come from? Was he one of the messengers sent by Sabirah? How had he gotten into her room?

"Are we — ?" He scratched his head and gestured toward her bare legs and the towel draped loosely around her middle. "Did we — ?" He squinted at her face, his gaze finally moving away from where her legs protruded from beneath the towel. "I'm sorry. Let me start over. Do I know you?"

Chapter Two

ຄ

William Moreland waited patiently for the woman's answer, but her mouth opened and closed a couple times before she managed to speak. For a moment he thought she might be a mute or stupid. Or maybe she didn't understand his language. He searched the fog of his brain for another language with which she might be familiar, but was spared the effort.

Still seated on the floor, her mouth finally formed words in English with an American accent. "No, you don't know me. And no, we didn't—" The woman's fluffy, white towel rose and fell with every breath she took, accentuating the curve of her breasts and the deep shadow of her cleavage. She certainly didn't look happy and her face was getting redder by the minute. Wasn't she satisfied? Women were always satisfied with his sexual performance.

And if they hadn't been making love, why was she lying on the floor in nothing more than a towel? For that matter, where the hell was he and who the hell was this woman? A quick glance around the room didn't help solve the mystery. The furniture was metal and fabric, unlike any he had ever seen in any hotel. The windows were wide expanses of glass surrounded by metal unlike the wood frames familiar to him. What was this place?

Cool air feathered across his skin and groin, alerting him to the fact he was totally naked in the company of a woman whose name he couldn't recall. "Hmm, this is a bit embarrassing." He cast his gaze around the room for something to cover himself with. But when he leaned toward a sofa to grab a loose pillow, the woman shot to her feet and crouched in a defensive position.

"Don't move or I'll have to hurt you."

Will froze in mid-reach. "Look, lady, I only want to cover myself so as not to offend you."

"I don't care what you want to do. Freeze, or else."

"God, I hate pushy broads."

"That's it, buddy, you're going down." She moved closer.

"What do you mean 'that's it'?" Will crossed his arms over his naked chest. If she wanted him to stay naked, so be it. "You think a little thing like you scares me?" He laughed, but his laugh was cut short when her bare foot connected with his rib cage.

Doubled over and the wind knocked from his lungs, he didn't see her hand chop down over his neck until too late. Will dropped to his knees and rolled to the side, away from the madwoman intent on killing him. As he rolled, he kicked out and clipped her shins, toppling her, towel and all, to the carpeted floor.

In seconds, he straddled her and trapped her hands above her head.

Feet flying, she struggled beneath him, her towel slipping off her bare breasts. But he didn't let go, nor did he apologize. He had a few questions he wanted answered before he let the hellcat loose.

"Who are you and why am I here?" he demanded.

She inhaled, calling more of his attention to those well-rounded breasts. "I asked you first."

With a smile, Will shook his head. "No you didn't."

"Then I should have!" She bucked beneath him, the towel sliding lower down her middle.

Will swallowed. The woman was entirely too nicely endowed and all that luscious skin was impacting his... *Stick to business, Will.* "You didn't answer me."

With her full lips thinned into a line, she answered, "I don't intend to, until you let me up."

"Oh, no. I'm not letting you up for a repeat performance. I'm sure I have a broken rib from the first time."

"Poor baby." She snorted and rocked to the left nearly unseating him.

"Keep it up, lady. I kinda like that." Probably more than he cared to admit and definitely more than he could hide.

The woman beneath him glanced at the evidence of her effect on him and gulped. Her movement ceased and her gaze lifted to his. "You're not going to..."

"Rape you?" Will laughed out loud. "Although you are tempting, I've never had to resort to force with my women. The ladies usually come willingly."

"Then let me be your first rejection." Her back arched and she pounded her bare feet against the floor. "Let...me...up."

"Not until you tell me who you are and why I'm here."

"Fine." With her brow furrowed into a frown, she said, "Kate Ralston."

"Now, was that so hard?"

Her brows rose. "You haven't let me go yet and I answered your question."

"You only answered one of my questions." His gaze kept slipping to her fully exposed breasts, the towel no longer covering so much as an inch of her body. A man could only take so much. Why didn't she demand to be covered? She must be very sure of herself, extremely frightened of him or a whore.

Was she a whore?

No, she didn't have that brassy, worn-down look he'd seen on the few ladies of the evening with whom he'd been acquainted. Will leaned toward self-assurance.

"Excuse me. My eyes are up here." And those blue eyes were icy.

"Couldn't help myself." He grinned. "You are truly blessed."

Her brows met over her nose. "Touch them and I'll break your fingers."

"Tsk, tsk." Will shook his head. "Pretty bold words for a woman trapped beneath a naked man."

"Look, if I knew why you were here, would I have attacked?"

"Maybe." Will almost chuckled aloud. Crafty little she-devil. She was using distraction as a method to draw his attention away from her exposed flesh. He frowned and racked his memory. "Last I recall I was in a filthy old tomb somewhere in the Zagros Mountains with Harry." He glanced at Kate. "Say, where's Harry?"

"How should I know where he is? I don't even know a Harry. Let me up!"

"You sure you didn't bring me here for some nefarious reason?"

"Positive. This is my hotel room and you're the intruder."

"Hmm, this is odd." He was getting entirely too aroused straddling the beautiful woman with all her black hair and those clear blue eyes. Maybe he'd better let her up. "Promise not to kick me again?"

"Yes, for heaven's sake."

"Well then, I guess you can get up." He rolled to the side and leaned over to stand.

Before he could climb to his feet, she was on top of him, slamming his face to the floor. "I see you have no honor," he muttered, with carpet digging into his cheek.

"And holding a woman against her will is honorable?" She held his arm up between his shoulder blades. "Why are you here?"

"I don't know."

"Convenient answer. Who's Harry? Or do you not know that either?"

"My partner. An archeologist on the same dig." Her bare bottom on his was doing crazy things to his already overactive libido. "Uh, do you think we could discuss this like two rational adults, maybe with clothing included?"

"Why should I give you that advantage when you didn't extend the same offer to me?"

Despite being flat on his belly and held in place by a woman, Will couldn't help smiling. She was sassy and he liked that in a woman. "You were the one who attacked me."

"You are the one who should be thrown in jail for breaking and entering. Who sent you? Sabirah?"

"I didn't force my way in here."

"Then what would you call it?"

"I don't know. One minute I was grabbing for that damned stone and the next, I'm waking up in your room with no clothing and a pain in the neck the size of a grown woman."

The woman on top of him tensed, her thighs clenching around his waist, her cunt pressing against his buttocks. "What stone?"

Will swallowed to lubricate his suddenly dry throat. Did she have any idea what she was doing to him? He'd been months without a woman's soft cunt to sink inside. "I don't know. Harry was excited by it. I was just along for the ride."

"What stone?" she asked again, her hand inching his arm up his back.

Pain speared through his arm. "Hey! Careful there, you'll break it." She loosened her hold a little. "Harry called it the Stone of Azhi or something like that."

When her thighs relaxed, Will swallowed his disappointment. Taut muscles encased in smooth-as-silk thighs were his favorite part of a woman's anatomy.

"I've heard of it." Her voice was quiet, not strong and vibrant like before.

"You sound disappointed."

"I said I've heard of it. I wasn't looking for it." She loosened her hold.

"What have you heard about it? Anything about where I can find Harry?" Will spit a dust bunny from his mouth. "Look, Kate, let me up and we can discuss this."

"How do I know you won't toss me to the floor like you did before?" Her fingers tightened, drawing his arm higher up his back.

Pain shot through his shoulder again and he bit down on his tongue to keep from yelling. "You don't," Will gritted between clenched teeth. "You might have to trust me."

"Trust a naked man?" She hesitated another minute before she moved from his back, leaving a little moisture in her wake, probably unaware of how incredibly sexy Will thought it was. At the moment, he had no intention of enlightening her, wincing as he touched his bruised rib.

Pull yourself together, William Moreland. She's a stranger. When he rolled over and sat up, he couldn't help but notice Kate staring at his cock.

While Kate wrapped the towel around herself, Will fought the urge to cover the object of her perusal with his hands. Why should he be embarrassed? She'd attacked him, not the other way around. Still, a gentleman didn't expose himself to a woman. Unless she asked. Her scrutiny only added to the problem as his cock surged higher. "Sorry. You were sitting on me with your bare bottom and I...well...couldn't help myself."

Her face flushed a bright red all the way to the tips of her ears. But she tossed her hair back in an overly careless pose. Her poise didn't last long, when she spoiled the whole effect by lunging for a pillow on the couch. "Jeez, cover yourself." She tossed the pillow at him, marched to the door and yanked it open. "And now, Mister…"

"Moreland. William Moreland." He didn't make a move toward the door.

"Do I have to call the hotel management to have you removed?"

"I'd be happy to remove myself, but I have a little problem." He glanced down at his body and back up with a grin. "I'm a bit exposed to go out on the streets."

"And your lack of clothing is a problem for me? I think not." She crossed her arms over her breasts. The movement emphasized her cleavage at the same time as it made the towel rise up her legs.

Will pressed the pillow to his groin. "Clothes would be nice. But I don't even know where I am."

She propped a fist on her hip. "Don't bullshit me, Bill."

"My friends call me Will."

"Will, Bill, whatever. Get out."

He moved, placing the couch between him and the doorway. "Not until I know what the hell's going on. Did you have me brought here?"

"Certainly not. I'm not that desperate that I have to pay to have a naked man brought to me."

"If you didn't bring me here and I don't remember how I got here…" He shook his head and glanced around the room. His gaze lit on the blue-green bottle on the coffee table. "Where did you get that?"

"What?"

"That bottle." He moved toward it.

"Why? Do you know anything about it?"

"Yes."

She closed the door and stalked toward him. "Then maybe you can tell me where the Eye of the Serpent is."

"I don't know anything about the Eye of the Serpent, but that bottle was in the sarcophagus with the dead princess."

"What sarcophagus? What princess?"

"In the tomb Harry and I were in. It's the last thing I remember. We both touched the Stone of Azhi and the next thing I know, I'm standing here without my clothes."

"You don't know anything about the Eye of the Serpent?"

He shrugged, holding tight to the pillow at his groin. "Nothing."

Kate snatched the bottle from the couch and shook it at him. "You didn't steal the Eye and replace it with this useless bottle?"

"No."

Her eyes narrowed into thin slits. "I don't trust you."

"I would never have guessed." Will couldn't help the grin spilling across his face. The woman was all spit and vinegar, unlike the usual placid types he went out with. And he liked it.

She walked to a desk against the wall and opened something that looked like a hard-shelled book. Instead of pages inside, there were keys like those on a typewriter.

"What's that?" Will asked.

"My laptop."

Huh? What the hell was she talking about? She was standing, therefore, she didn't have a lap. "I don't understand."

With a narrow-eyed glare shot back at him, she pressed a key and a picture appeared in brilliant color.

Will's heart leaped into his throat and he jumped backward. "What did you just do? How is this possible?"

Again, she glanced at him, her brows furrowing. "You're kidding me, right?"

"About what?" He inched toward the strange contraption. "It's like a photograph with lights behind it." Leaning forward, he looked behind the black box. No lights shone through. "How did you do that?"

"You are strange." She shrugged and pressed several keys.

The picture changed to a screen with a word he didn't recognize. "What is G.O.O.G.L.E?"

"Google." She clicked on the keys and words appeared in a little box. "Don't tell me you don't know about Google?"

"Okay, I won't tell you." He watched as the picture changed and an entire list of words and names appeared. Amazed and bewildered, he stepped back. "What are you doing?"

"I'm going to the Internet to look up information on the Stone of Azhi."

Was the woman speaking Greek or some other foreign language? Will scratched his head and dared her wrath to ask. "What's the Internet?"

"Quit pulling my leg, Will. I'm only humoring you because you're so pathetic." She turned and gave him that look again. "And don't try anything funny."

Will decided it would be better if he didn't display his ignorance. But the black box with the bright pictures fascinated him. He'd never in his life seen such a thing. It was almost like a motion picture, only in color.

Kate's hands paused over the keys. "Don't you own your own laptop?"

"No."

"You'd think that by 2005, everyone would have a laptop. You can do so much with one."

"Two thousand and five what?" The more Kate talked, the more Will was convinced she was speaking in some weird dialect. He only understood about half of what she was saying.

"What do you mean?" she asked, her attention on the picture, her fingers clicking against the keys.

"Two thousand and five what? Dollars, bottles of wine, paving stones, people? I don't understand."

"The year." She planted her hands on her terrycloth-covered hips. "Did you just fall off a turnip truck or something?"

"Are you trying to tell me this is the year 2005?" He stepped backward, laughter bubbling up in his throat.

"Of course. It follows 2004."

Unable to contain it longer, Will burst out laughing, clutching his side with his free hand. "For a moment I though you believed it. Everyone knows it's 1924."

Kate stared at him like he'd grown a third ear. "1924? Why would it be 1924?"

Ringing filled his ears and he staggered to the sofa dropping down on its edge. The pillow forgotten, he buried his head in his hands. "I don't feel very well."

"Great, now I'll have a sick, naked man camped out on my couch. How do you spell the name of that stone?"

Will closed his eyes and prayed the dizziness would go away. "Azhi—A.Z.H.I, I think."

Soft clicking sounded from the corner where Kate stood, but Will couldn't lift his head. What had gone wrong? If she were telling the truth, where had he been for the past eighty years? Why did he still look like he did in 1924?

His head jerked up and he stared at his arms, still darkly tanned and muscular, not that of a hundred-and-five-year-old man. "This is the year two thousand and five?" he asked again.

"Yes." Kate didn't look up from the bright pictures.

"I've got a bigger problem than I originally thought."

Her hands hovered over the keys as she read the words on the picture. "You sure do."

"What do you mean?"

"Says here, the Stone of Azhi was a magical stone placed in the sarcophagus of Vashti, the Devil King's daughter, to protect her spirit from evil men. Any man who touches the stone will be imprisoned in one of the bottles found with the princess until a woman awakens him. At which time, he will be required to grant her every wish."

"What?" Will stood, grabbed the pillow and strode across the room. "What kind of rubbish is that anyway?"

"It's an ancient curse. I don't know if there's any truth to it. I have to admit, I didn't believe in magic until my father disappeared a year ago. One day he was in the desert with a Bedouin tribe, the next day he had disappeared. So, normally I'd say this curse business was a bunch of bunk. But if it means I get what I wish for, I'm willing to give it a try." A wicked grin spirited itself across her face. "If you really did touch the Stone of Azhi and were imprisoned in that bottle, I should be able to wish for anything I want."

Will snorted. "If you believe in fairy tales."

She laughed out loud. "This could be interesting. I wish you were fully clothed in an Elvis Presley outfit."

"Who's Elvis Presley?" As the words left Will's mouth, the floor shook and thunder rumbled through the room.

"You'd think this was California, as much movin' and shakin's goin' on," Kate shouted as she held on to the desk.

Will blinked his eyes, and in just that short a span of time, his body was covered with fabric. "Huh?"

"Ohmigod!" Kate's eyes widened and she burst out laughing. "Ohmigod!"

"What?" he demanded.

"Look at you!"

"What?" Will spun, prepared to defend himself from some unseen attacker. No one was back there. "What?" Then Will glanced down at the white shiny clothing covering his skin. When he lifted his arm, fringe hung down to his waist and rhinestones sparkled from his ankles up to his chin. "How'd these clothes get on me?"

Kate's laughter died down to intermittent fits of giggles. "I don't know…but you're…hysterical!"

"I fail to see humor in this…this…clown suit." But the more Kate giggled, the more Will's lips twitched. "Well, it might be a little funny." A chuckle burbled up his throat and he joined her belly laughs until his sides hurt.

Kate sat up, her laughter halting, her eyes wide. "Ohmigod. I wished you into those clothes. Do you realize what this means?" Her gaze took on a calculating gleam.

"I don't like that look in your eyes." He glowered at her. "Damn, where's Harry?"

* * * * *

Somewhere in Iraq, 2005

The dark-skinned Syrian poked an AK-47 in Harry Taylor's chest and spoke in broken English, "Why you here? You spy for Americans?"

Harry only shook his head and mumbled through the filthy rag stuffed in his mouth. How did the idiot expect him to answer with his mouth full of cloth? Even without the cloth, what would the guy expect? "Yeah, I'm a spy, so what's it to you?" Or he could tell the truth. "No, I'm here looking for some friends of mine. You seen a couple guys named Will and Mitch? They're trapped inside glass bottles, you know, the ones you hear about in genie stories? I'm here to rescue them." Who'd believe him?

Besides, the man with the gun looked like he had the sense of humor of a rabid dog. As the thought surfaced, the butt of the dog's weapon slammed against Harry's temple.

Bright lights swam in circles around Harry's face, as he tipped over. With his hands tied behind his back, he was unable to cushion his fall. He hit the hard-packed earth with his left shoulder, the jolt reverberating throughout his body.

The dog jerked the cloth from his mouth and Harry gasped for precious air, choking on a nose full of desert dust. Coughing, he fought to sit upright. "Where's Edie?" he demanded. "Where's the woman?"

Once again, metal encased in hard plastic met bone encased in soft flesh and Harry groaned. How did he get in this situation and where was Edie? *Must stay awake and find Edie.* He fought the dizziness but soon slipped into painless oblivion.

Chapter Three

ꙮ

A flood of adrenaline flushed through Kate's veins. "If the legend is true. I can wish for anything."

Will frowned, not sure he liked what she was saying. "Are you serious? Do you really believe in magic?"

The rush of excitement paled. Did she believe in magic? Hadn't she been racing around the world for the past year to find a magical stone to free her father from Sand City? Was the truth staring her in the face all along? Had her father perished in the desert and she was chasing sand castles in the sky to find him? She leveled a stare at Will. "Hell yes, I believe in magic."

"You might, but I don't." He paced across the room, apparently unaware of how sexy his backside was in the rhinestone-studded, skintight white pants. Elvis never looked *this* fine.

Kate sat down in the chair by the laptop and crossed her legs, not that crossing her legs stopped her purely instinctive reaction to fine male flesh paraded in front of her. If she wasn't mistaken, he'd originally thought they'd slept together. She tipped her head to the side. Well, he wasn't the kind of guy she usually slept with, but then none of them made her hot like this one did without even trying.

He spun, his gaze catching hers.

Kate's cheeks warmed.

"There has to be another explanation." His eyes closed to slits. "Are you sure Harry didn't put you up to this?"

"Harry, your partner?"

"Yes. If not Harry, who would put you up to such an elaborate hoax?"

"I could say the same." She stood and walked over to stop in front of him. "You almost had me going over the laptop, but how do I know Toad-the-Sleaze didn't put you up to mischief to distract me from killing him?"

"Toad? You know a guy named Toad?"

"Yeah, unfortunately." Her blood burned at the deception. "Todd and Sabirah have the Eye of the Serpent, which I paid for and didn't receive."

"I don't know anything about the Eye of the Serpent or whatever, but I would like to know what the hell is going on. And how do you explain this outlandish outfit?"

Kate crossed her arms. "Maybe it sounds crazy but let's run with the magic theory."

"You've got to be out of your mind."

"I don't see you coming up with anything better." Damn him and his superior attitude. "If you aren't willing to test the magic, then I will."

"Oh, no you don't. If it should work, how do I know you won't use it to hurt me again?"

Her brows rose. "Did I hurt with my wish to clothe you?"

Will's brows dipped. "No."

"What's the matter? You think I'll do something stupid, Elvis Boy?" She glanced at his body, enjoying the faint flush spreading up his neck into his cheeks.

He lifted his arms, the long white fringe spreading like a bird's wings. "You don't think this is stupid?"

"Elvis made a fortune in it."

"Good for Elvis. Either the circus is paying much better, or he must have been a very good clown."

"How about something easy like, I wish you were naked and that you'd fuck me like a whore? Would that make you happy?"

The room shook and thunder rumbled, rattling the windows.

"Damn, there must be a storm nearby. That's the third time that's happened in the past thirty minutes." Kate walked over to the windows to stare out onto the city of Riyadh. Not a cloud marred the clear blue sky. "Can you have thunder without clouds?"

Arms encircled her waist and pulled her up against a solid wall of muscles. "Hey!"

Before she could react, lips descended on the curve of her neck and a tongue laved the skin. Her knees buckling, Kate held on to the curtains to steady herself before she turned to face Will.

He'd shed his Elvis outfit and stood as naked as when he'd shown up in her room. His light blue eyes had deepened almost to midnight as he stepped closer, his hardened cock pressing into the towel covering Kate's belly.

Blood thundered in her ears. "What are you doing?"

"I'm about to fuck you like a whore." One hand slid around her neck and tipped her head back, exposing her mouth, throat and lips to him. The other hand grabbed the end of the towel. In one tug, he ripped it from her body and tossed it across the room.

"Will! Stop it right now!"

"I can't seem to do that. You're absolutely irresistible."

Adrenaline surged through her body heightening her awareness of every one of his attributes melding against hers. "Stop, William Moreland," she said in a breathy voice, "or I'll have to hurt—"

He captured her mouth with his and she could no longer think. She exploded in a disgusting array of sensations like a multicolored firecracker. Unable to stop him and quickly not caring, she returned his kiss, tongue to tongue, breast to chest.

When Will's lips finally broke contact, Kate sagged against him. Thankful he'd stopped before she begged him to go further.

Her gratitude was short-lived when Will's work-roughened hands slid up her waist to cup her breasts, kneading the tender flesh until her nipples puckered into tight little buds.

Liquid desire rushed downward, coating the entrance to her pussy. She wanted him inside her. Now!

He was a stranger and she wanted him inside her. Kate didn't know this man from Adam and she knew the danger of fucking a stranger. He could be a murderer, a thief or a crazy man. The very uncertainty made her pussy weep all the more.

When Will leaned down to suck one of her breasts into his mouth, Kate moaned long and low.

His tongue twisted and teased her nipple until Kate squirmed. "The other, please. Do the other."

"Patience, my dear. There's more where that came from."

As he switched his mouth from one breast to the other, his hand slid down to the curly mound at the juncture between her thighs.

Kate's mind screamed, *Danger! Warning! Do not pass go! Do not collect—*

Before she could respond to the warning, his fingers parted her folds and slipped inside her wet entrance, dipping and stroking.

Her tension built and stretched until she thought she would explode. "Will, you're killing me," she gasped.

"There's more where that came from," he repeated with a smile and then kneeled, slowly trailing his lips and free hand down her body. He paused to dip his tongue into her bellybutton and tangle his fingers in the curly hair over her mons. When his mouth lowered still further and he pressed a kiss to her inner thigh, Kate gasped and her pussy creamed.

Oh, he was not going down on her, was he? This is the part where Kate should call a halt to the madness. Fire raced through her veins and she couldn't bring herself to stop him. Desire overruled and she slid her ass up on the windowsill, parting her legs to let him in.

"I'm acting like a fucking slut," she said, her head dropping back against the cool, glass window. "My father would wash my mouth out with soap for that. And I don't give a damn."

Will's fingers slid inside her. One...then two...then three...stretching her, his fingers long and tapered but not long enough to fill her. "More, please. More."

"Are you begging me?" He nipped her inner thigh. "Beg me, Kate."

"Never." He parted her folds and tongued her clit once.

Her body convulsed and she grabbed his hair. "Please. I beg you."

"That's more like it." He smiled and leaned forward, sucking her entire clit into his mouth, the strong pressure piercing through her bringing her to the edge. Then he flicked her with his tongue at the same time he shoved all four fingers inside.

Kate burst over the edge, her hands digging into his scalp, alternating between pushing him away and pulling him back to do more of that magic he did.

For several minutes she lay plastered against the window, satiated yet not complete.

Will stood and moved between her legs. "Did you like that?"

"You couldn't tell?"

He kissed her lips, his mouth still tasting of her juices. The thought stirred her limp body back to life.

"Tell me you're not done?"

"Oh no. Not by a long shot." With a wicked grin, he grabbed her beneath her ass and pulled her away from the window. Will wrapped her legs around his waist and eased her downward until her cunt hovered over the tip of his rock-hard cock.

41

"You want it?" He nudged her opening and nipped at her breast.

"Oh, yes," she moaned.

"Then tell me."

Desire flushed her body. "I want it."

"No, tell me like a whore."

"Fuck me, already."

He lunged upward at the same time he pulled her down over him, filling her until she thought he would ram right through her body.

Kate screamed.

Will backed out, immediately. "Did I hurt you?"

"Oh God no!" She pushed herself back down over him and rocked up and down. "This feels so fucking good."

Will matched thrust for thrust. Then he pulled her up and off, setting her on her feet.

The shock of going from fever pitch to sudden emptiness made Kate want to screech with dissatisfaction. "Why'd you do that? Why'd you stop?"

"Because I'm going to fuck you like this." He spun her around so fast, she grabbed for the windowsill.

"Ever wonder what a bitch feels like when a dog fucks her?"

Desperate to have him back inside her, what little was left of Kate's inhibitions blew out the window. "Oh yes. Do it!"

Will grabbed her ass, ran his hand down between her cheeks until he found her opening. The coarse skin of his fingers ignited the sensitive nerve endings and her pussy quivered, ready and waiting for the humping he promised her.

And Will didn't disappoint. He rammed into her in one hard thrust, stretching here until she thought she'd die from pleasure.

"Like that, bitch?"

"Shut up and fuck me, you mangy beast." Was that her mouth saying those raunchy words? Had she lost her fucking mind?

He leaned over her and nipped her neck. Then he pumped in and out of her, his balls slapping against her thighs.

When he stiffened, she knew he was going to come.

But he stopped and reached around to strum her clit until she wanted to weep. With one final thrust, she shattered into a thousand pieces. Will filled her, his cock jerking and throbbing inside her pussy.

"I think I'm going to die," Kate whispered.

"Not yet, we still have round two."

"Round two? Good lord, I will die."

He pulled his cock free and dropped to his knees behind her to tongue her wet, creamy pussy.

"Please, Will, I don't think I can take it again. I wish you'd stop."

The floor shook and thunder rumbled.

Kate dropped to her knees beside Will.

As quickly as it had begun, the shaking ceased.

Will sat staring at her naked body like he was in some kind of trance. Then he shook his head. "What the hell happened?"

"There was some kind of earthquake or something."

"No, not that…" He waved at her naked form and his and then his hand went to his mouth still slick with her juices. "Did we just do what I think we did?"

Kate frowned. "You mean to tell me you don't remember fucking me like a dog?"

His eyes widened. "Oh my God, did I?" He shook his head. "My apologies. I don't know what came over me. I've never fuck—made love to a woman like she was an animal."

"You're not pulling my leg, are you?" She pushed against him. "I mean, you were going at it like you knew what you were doing. I thought you wanted to do it." Her face warmed and then her eyes widened. "Oh shit."

"What?"

"The wish."

"What are you talking about?"

"I wished you'd fuck me like a whore."

"You did what?" Will shouted.

Kate shot to her feet and planted her fists on her naked hips. "I was testing a theory."

"I'd say your test proved your theory."

"You mean you didn't do it because you wanted to?" Her chest tightened at the thought.

"One minute we were arguing, the next minute my body took over and I can't do a thing about it." He glanced down at his glistening cock, lying flaccid against his leg.

"Talk about a blow to the ego." Jeez. *How did you face the man you more or less raped on a wish?*

"Not that I didn't enjoy it." He grinned. "On the contrary, it was…animalistic."

So much for feeling sorry for the guy. Kate grabbed the pillow he'd discarded and shoved it into his chest. "Great. Now you'll think I'm a fucking animal."

Disregarding the discarded towel, Kate stalked across the room, naked and not giving a damn.

Will caught up with her and grabbed her arm. "Kate, you're beautiful and whether or not I fu—made love to you of my own will, I'm grateful.

"Of all the stupid, insensitive, moronic things a guy could say—"

The wind was knocked from her sails when Will's lips descended over hers, shutting off the stream of epithets she was ready to sling at him.

Despite her resolve to throw him out at the first chance she got, Kate melted into his arms and returned his kiss.

When they broke apart, she gathered enough wind to say, "Don't think you won that argument."

He gave her a purely superior, male smile. "I think my talents have proven themselves."

"Oh, so now you're the cocky one?" She raised her eyebrows and glanced at the pillow held in front of his penis. "I have the power to wish, you have to grant my wishes. I wouldn't push me."

"Don't push you?" Will stalked across the room his ire rising with each step he took on the lush carpet emphasizing his nakedness. "Are you Daddy's little girl used to getting her way at the expense of others? Good God, Kate, who died and made you princess of the world?"

Her eyes widened and the proud and adventurous Kate whose eyes flashed fire a moment before glistened with a film of unshed tears.

She met him halfway across the floor and poked her finger in his chest. "He is not dead. Do you hear me? Not!" On that final word, she turned, walked into the bedroom shutting the door between them.

On the other side of the panel she continued to talk, the words muffled and hard to understand.

"Now what?" Will asked the empty room. Without Kate in it, he was at a loss and not liking it. "If you really can make wishes come true you could at least wish me some decent clothing," he shouted through the panel.

More muttering sounded from within and then the building rocked. As thunder rattled the windows, Will felt his skin tingle. When he looked down, he had the damned clown suit on again.

"Just who the hell is Elvis, some freak in a sideshow?" he yelled at the panels of the closed door.

The door crashed open and Kate stood there wearing what looked like a black, sleeveless undershirt and khaki pants and carrying a brush. Her hair hung down around her shoulders and the fire was back in her eyes. "Elvis was the king."

"King of what? Ringling Brothers Barnum and Bailey Circus?" He had a hard time concentrating on the conversation when there was still so much of Kate's arms and shoulders to see beneath the slip of a shirt.

"What do you know? If you really are from, what was it, 1924, you wouldn't have a clue."

"I am and I don't. Enlighten me."

As Kate raked the brush through her hair, she explained, "Elvis was the king of rock and roll, a new era in music that changed everything."

"Interesting. And did you know Elvis personally?"

"No, he died before I was born."

"Then why did you say he wasn't dead?"

"I wasn't talking about Elvis." She turned away from him and strapped a knife to her forearm.

"If you weren't talking about Elvis who had your knickers all in a twist?"

"Oooh!" She faced him with the knife pointed at his chest. "I did not have my knickers in a twist."

"Did too." Will pushed the knife aside. "Be careful where you point that. And tell me that isn't all you're going to wear. Do all women go around partially clothed and wearing men's trousers?"

With a deep breath, she blew air out her nose like an angry bull. "I wish you'd go to Hell, Will."

"Please tell me you didn't wish me to go to Hell." He grimaced and waited. As expected, the floor beneath him rolled. "I don't have a good feeling about this."

"Too bad. You pissed me—"

Before Kate finished her sentence, Will's world went black.

* * * * *

Will staggered through a blisteringly hot, red desert. The wind blew at hurricane force, blasting him with sand and ash. Everything, including the air he breathed, burned like fire. The white fringe hanging from his arms burst into flame. As he flapped around like a bird, his eyebrows started smoking. Alternating between flapping and slapping his eyebrows, Will yelled into the sand-filled gusts, "Harry, what have you gotten me into?"

* * * * *

"Harry? Harry! Oh, God, don't die on me, Harry."

Light edged between his eyelids and he glanced up into the face of a frizzy, red-haired angel. Had he died and gone to heaven? He glanced at the four dirty walls surrounding them. No, he was still in the same room the guard had dumped him in when they'd been brought bound and gagged to the compound. "Edie? Edie Ragsdale? How'd you get in here?"

"I wished myself here. Can you sit up?"

"Wished?" His vision wobbled and then focused on the woman he'd grown to love in a very short time. Edie. The person who'd freed him from a bottle several days ago, launching him into a wild chase across the world to find his two friends caught in the same predicament.

She tugged at his arm. "Hurry, Harry."

"I'm getting there. It would help if you could untie my hands."

When Edie loosened the ropes behind him, blood rushed into his hands like so many acupuncture needles, setting his fingers on fire. He pushed himself into a sitting position and his head swam. "Where are Mitch and Will?"

"I don't know, probably a hundred miles from here by now. The truck left, but we've been stuck in this compound for two days."

"It's been that long?" He tried to shake the wool out of his head, but only managed to make his head ache.

"Yes, it has. Which reminds me…" Edie stood, planted her hands on her hips and stared down at him. "Harry, if we're going to have any kind of a relationship, you're going to have to trust me."

He had a hard time focusing on her standing so far above him and his head was pounding like Indian tom-toms. He blinked up at her, appreciating the curve of her hip and the swell of her breasts even through the fog of pain. "I trust you, Edie."

"Good, because the next time I tell you to shoot, shoot!"

A vague recollection of a pistol being slipped into his hand in the dark surfaced through the fog of his throbbing brain. He'd been so amazed that his mousy museum worker had brought a gun, he'd waited too long to use it. Thus the incarceration in an Iraqi insurgent's camp and being trussed up like a pig waiting to be roasted. Oh boy, his head hurt. He pressed a hand to his temple and winced.

A shout sounded somewhere in the building.

Harry's heart slammed into his gut. "Uh, Edie?"

She combed her fingers through his hair. "Yes, Harry?"

With a wince, he moved his sore head away from her well-intentioned fingers. "Could we continue this conversation somewhere else?"

"Oh, yeah. Maybe that would be a good idea." Edie glanced over her shoulder. "I think they've figured out I'm not in my cell. Come on, we have to get out of here." She draped one of his arms over her shoulder and helped him to his feet.

Booted footsteps pounded down the hallway toward their little piece of Hell.

Just as keys jangled in the lock on the other side of the door, Edie calmly said, "I wish we were out of this compound."

As the familiar sound of thunder echoed against the walls, the room shook and Harry braced himself. Ever since Edie had freed him from the bottle, he'd been forced to grant her wishes. Okay, so forced wasn't exactly the right word. He couldn't stop the wishes from coming true. So, when Edie made her wishes...well, Harry had learned to hold his breath. Invariably a catastrophe was about to take place. "I don't know about this, Edie. Your wishes never quite turn out right."

More shouting sounded on the other side of the door and Edie cocked an eyebrow at him. "It's better than being stuck in here, isn't it?"

Harry wasn't so sure, but before he could answer, his world went black.

* * * * *

Kate walked across the rug, gnawing on her fingernail. Where had Will gone? One minute they were arguing...and damned if she was kind of enjoying it...the next he was gone. Could he really be in Hell?

She planted her fists on her hips. Well, the jerk deserved it, thinking he was all that. Contradicting everything she said. None of her family or the people on her staff contradicted her. They didn't dare. Hadn't she gotten by on her own for over a year? Of course, he wasn't one of her staff and she did wish him to do all those wonderful things he did to her. If he'd been in his right mind, he probably would never have fucked her like a whore. No man had ever fucked her like a whore.

A shiver of remembered pleasure tickled its way across her flesh. She liked being treated like trash. It got her off in a big way. Her hand traveled down over her breasts and down inside her pants to the place Will had licked so thoroughly. Wow. She was wet just thinking about him.

And he was burning in Hell?

Damn it!

"I wish Will back here, now!"

The room shook and Kate lurched to the side. As thunder boomed, she steadied herself her breath coming in short, shallow gasps.

Where was Will?

She blinked and he stood before her, his blue eyes smoking.

No, not his eyes — his eyebrows were smoking!

"Ohmigod!" She reached out and stubbed her thumb against his eyebrow to stop the smoke and jerked it away when it burned her. "Yikes! You really are a hunka-hunka burnin' love. Will, what happened?"

"What happened?" Will blew in and out through his nose like a prize bull in a bullfighting ring.

Kate cringed and tried a shaky smile. "Did you really go...you know..."

"To Hell?" He glanced down at his singed body hair and the stubs of fringe emitting a really nasty odor. "What do you think?"

"I'm so sorry." She threw her arms around him and realized too late how badly burned skin must hurt.

Will yelped and shoved her away.

Kate bit her fingernail, at a loss for the first time in her life. She'd actually hurt someone who didn't really deserve it. Well, not this badly, anyway. "Oh hell, I wish you weren't hurt."

"Kate, did you make a wish with the word Hell in it?"

"Yes, I did, but—"

"I'm doomed." As the floor shook yet again, Will rolled his eyes to the ceiling. "Why can't you leave me alone? Haven't you done enough—"

As thunder rumbled, Will's skin changed from the angry red to its normal desert tan, unscarred, no burns and his eyebrows no longer smoked! He was back to his normal, uncooked state, pre-Hell state.

Will tested his eyebrows. He still wore the singed clown suit as proof he'd really been to Hell. But other than that, he looked fine.

Kate's chest tightened as he stared at her.

"If that was your idea of funny, I'm leaving." He spun and headed for the door.

How could she let the best sex she'd ever had walk out the door? She beat him to it and blocked his escape with her body. "I said I was sorry." She laid a hand on his arm. "Please, don't go."

"I can't take being fried like an egg again."

"I promise. It won't happen again." Was that her voice pleading? Kate never pleaded. What was it about this man?

Sex. The extreme fucking she'd done with this stranger was unbelievably unforgettable and it had turned her brain to mush.

Will's eyes narrowed into slits. "I don't trust you."

"I know, but think of the possibilities of the wishes." She grabbed his hand and ushered him away from the door. "We could find your friend Harry, and I could find the Eye of the Serpent."

"I can find Harry on my own," he said, stubbornly refusing to get over his anger. Not that Kate could blame him. He'd been a flaming, human torch!

"Please, Will. I need to find the Eye. It's a matter of life and death."

"Your life, my death?" He shook his head. "No. I'm leaving." He picked her up and set her to the side and opened the door.

"Will." Okay, so begging hadn't worked. She dropped that pleading from her voice and in its place was the regular Kate used to getting her way. The one who'd argued with Will before she sent him to Hell.

Will paused and turned back to look at her. "What?"

"You're forgetting something."

"Oh yes." He walked back across the room and grabbed the blue-green bottle. "Don't know if I'll need this to find Harry."

"That wasn't what I was referring to," she said.

"I don't know what you're talking about. I arrived with nothing else."

"There is the matter of the wishes."

Kate could tell when understanding dawned. First his eyes widened, then narrowed. "No. You will not force me to be a slave to your wishes. I refuse."

Her arms crossed over her chest and her lips curled upward. "I don't think you have much of a choice."

"I'm leaving and you can't stop me." He strode through the door and closed it firmly behind him.

The floor pitched beneath his feet and he slammed against the wall. When he heard thunder, he closed his eyes and groaned.

Chapter Four

ॐ

Standing in the middle of the insurgent compound wasn't Harry's idea of a safer place to be than the cell they'd just left. "Edie, wish us the hell out of here, quick. No wait. Be more specific. Wish us to where Will is."

A shout sounded from around the side of a building and shots were fired.

Edie clenched her eyes shut and said, "I wish Harry and I were where Will is, now!"

Five armed terrorists charged around the corner with their guns pointed at Edie and Harry.

"Hurry up, magic. Hurry!" As a round kicked up the dust at his feet, Harry threw himself in front of Edie just as blessed oblivion consumed them.

* * * * *

Kate paced the sitting area of her hotel suite, awaiting Will's return. She wished he would hurry so she could put her thoughts into action. When Will's body materialized, she breathed a sigh. "Good, you're back." Then she saw Will's face, and she winced.

He did not look in the least happy about being pulled back into her room.

"Oh, be a big boy and get over it," she said.

"There's nothing to get over. I'm not staying."

"You are and you're going to help me find the Eye of the Serpent." She held up her hand when he opened his mouth. "Once we find the Eye, I'll help you find your partner."

"Assuming I'll help you."

She propped a hand on her hip. "Honey, you don't have a choice."

"Great, I'm shackled to a pushy b—"

"Don't." She got right in his face and poked his chest with her finger.

"Don't what?"

"Don't call me a broad."

He captured her finger and held on so tight she couldn't get away. "I'll call you what I please."

"I wish you would never call me a broad again."

Will opened his mouth, his lips forming into the shape necessary to emit a B and he said, "Bunny."

Kate laughed. "Good. That fixes that."

"Witch, pest, brat, bitch." He flung his hand out. "Are you going to wish the man right out of me?" He strode for the door. "I'm leaving. I'd rather be dead than stay."

"Okay, okay. I wish you could call me a broad again."

"Broad." A smile slid up his face and he fixed her with a hard stare. "Look, broad, I don't want to play in your sandbox. I have a friend out there that could use my help. I'm not going to play around looking for some bauble with you."

"That bauble may mean the difference between life and death for my father."

"What do you mean?"

She sighed and sat on the edge of the couch. "It's a long story."

"Give me the short version."

"My father is an engineer who also has a love of archeology. He was on a humanitarian mission to the desert to help one of the Bedouin tribes with their water needs when he stumbled upon a legend he couldn't resist."

"Were you with him?"

"No, I was attending university, finishing up my master's so I didn't get to go on this trip. But he sent letters and described what he was doing." Kate twisted her fingers together.

"I take it his search lead to problems?"

"I got letters from him at least once a month and he promised he'd be back for my graduation. But when the time came, he didn't come."

"No letters explaining?"

"None. I flew from California to Riyadh—"

"Wait a minute, flew?" An eyebrow climbed up his forehead. "I don't recall seeing any wings on your body a while ago."

"You really are from 1924." She laughed. "People can take trips in airplanes now. Huge airplanes that will hold hundreds."

"Amazing." Will sat next to her on the couch. "Has everything changed that much since 1924?"

"You have no idea." Kate snorted softly. "We've even been to the moon and back."

"You have?" His eyes widened and his mouth dropped open.

"Not me personally, but other Americans and Russians have flown in ships to space and the moon."

Will shook his head. "This is too much to even comprehend."

"No kidding." She could show and tell him so many more astounding changes. "But back to the story."

"Yes, yes. Please go on."

"When I found the Bedouin tribe, they said he'd discovered Sand City. Despite the tribe's warning, he trekked in and, from their accounts, the legendary city consumed him."

"Consumed? As in ate?"

Kate shrugged. "More or less."

"Are you sure that wasn't their way of saying he was buried alive in a sandstorm?"

Her brows furrowed. "At first I thought that. I stayed with the Bedouin for several weeks, caught up in my grief, thinking my father was dead. But the longer I stayed the more I learned. Sand City was cursed by an ancient Devil King."

"Like Harry's?"

"Yes. Maybe the same one. Anyway, the king was angry because the prince of Sand City broke the heart of the Devil King's daughter.

"In retribution, the Devil King stole the Eye of the Serpent. To keep any of the inhabitants from coming to claim it, he cursed the city and made it disappear. Not only were they made invisible, the people living there couldn't leave the city. All who accidentally or intentionally enter the city could never come out. With the city lost to sight, the only thing that can help outsiders find it is Sand City's sacred jewel, the Eye of the Serpent. Without it, the city is supposed to be impossible to find."

"But your father found it?"

"The Bedouin think he stumbled into it on one of his quests to locate it. Now that he's there, he can't get out."

"Let me get this right, you want to find this city and go inside to be with your father and never come out?"

"Yes and no. The legend also said that if the Eye is returned to the sacred statue within the city, the curse will be lifted, and everyone will be free to leave if they wish."

"So, you need to find the Eye to find your father."

"And free him." Kate stared down at her hands clasped in her lap. "I love my father very much and he's all the family I have left in the world." There, she'd spilled her guts, told her story, now all she could do was pray Will would help her. Because even if he didn't want to, she'd use her wishes to find her father anyway. She hazarded a glance at Will, a man she'd known for less than an hour. A man she'd put her faith in to help her find her father.

Please let him find it in his heart to help me.

Will turned and paced a few steps away before facing her again. "Assuming I help you in this crazy scheme to free a hidden city from a curse, you promise you'll help me find my friend and lift this crazy spell I seem to be under?"

Hope stirred in her heart and Kate sat forward. "Yes."

"And you won't wish me to make love to you. That's somewhat hard on a man's ego. I like to be in control of what I'm doing."

Not wish him to fuck her like a whore? Kate worried her lip with her teeth. She'd never enjoyed sex more with a man. "Do I have to promise that?"

"Yes, or no deal."

Give up the sex? Whew, Kate never thought that would be a tough decision. But then she'd never had sex with a man like Will. "I could make you help me with or without your agreement."

"It would be easier to have my support, don't you think?" He strode across the carpeted floor to stand directly in front of her, his shoulders consuming her view.

Kate's mouth went dry and she whispered, "No sex?"

"Not unless I initiate it." He lifted her chin with his finger, his lips hovering within a breath of hers. "I'm actually quite good at initiating."

"Really?" she said, looking up into his bluer than blue eyes. How did he manage to make her a mushy, limp-kneed teenager with just a look?

Those full, sensuous lips brushed over hers while his hand swept up her waistline beneath her tank top to cup a full, straining breast, a thumb rubbing over the pebbled nipple. "Really." One step closer and his cock pressed into her belly through his trousers and hers, the heat setting her pussy awash with need and come.

It was all she could do to keep from wishing him to take her and fuck her like a whore again. Kate clamped down hard on her tongue until tears sprang to her eyes.

Will eased her shirt upward, exposing her lacy black bra. Leaning forward he pressed a kiss to each mound, slipping fingers around the back to unhook the catch, freeing her breasts.

Kate's back arched, pressing her breasts closer to his tantalizing lips. "I wish—"

"Uh-uh." Will touched a finger to her lips, halting further flow of words and he leaned forward to suck her nipple into his mouth, tonguing the tip.

A moan escaped her throat as she shamelessly threaded her fingers through his blond hair, tugging him closer. Her calf slid up the back of his leg, tugging him closer until her cunt rested against his thigh and she rode him. Her pussy ached and she wanted to be naked so bad it hurt.

Will's hand slid down her belly and snapped open her jeans, sliding the zipper down. Strong, broad fingers slipped inside and strummed her clit until she sang, crying out his name for all the world to hear beyond the hotel room walls.

"Want more?"

"Oh, yes, please," she said, sagging against him, pressing his hand to her pussy. Eager to be naked, she pushed her jeans down over her hips and stepped out of them.

When Will laughed, she refused to be put off. Instead, she grabbed for the button of his trousers and yanked the button open, pulling the zipper down with more enthusiasm than care.

"Careful now," he said, covering her hand with his.

"I'm on fire. I wi—"

The finger on her lip forced her to think about her words. "I *want* you to fuck me. Now!"

"In my own time, darlin'. In my own time," Will said. Scooping his hand behind her ass, he lifted her off her feet and wrapped her legs around his waist. "I'm of the opinion there are better places than the floor to do this proper."

With her clit rubbing the ridge of his fly, Kate couldn't fight the rise of tension in her pussy. "The bed! Get to the bed! Oh jeez, make it soon."

Laughing, he carried her to the bedroom and laid her out on the coverlet. When he tried to stand up straight, her legs tightened, holding him over her.

"I'm not going very far," he said, loosening her legs from his waist and laying them over the edge of the bed. "I'm not done, yet."

Reluctantly, she let him rise. He leaned across her, his chest pressing against hers as he reached for a pillow.

"Please don't tell me you're going to sleep."

"On the contrary." He dragged the pillow across the bed and shoved it beneath her hips. "Sleep is the farthest thing from my mind." Then he dropped between her legs and draped them over her shoulders. "I have a little more initiation to do." Then his tongue found her clit and stroked her gently, his fingers parting her folds, opening her up to his mouth. Moving lower, he tongued her pussy, pushing into her wet channel and flicking the walls of her vagina until she squirmed for more.

Her pussy gushed, aching to be filled with his cock. Her fingers knotted in the sheets and she howled, "Please, I want you inside me. Please!"

"Almost there," he said and pulled away, climbing to his feet.

Kate could have wept as her pussy cooled. "You can't stop now. You just can't."

"Who said I was?" His hands grasped her hips and he flipped her over to her stomach, the pillow lodged beneath her hips, making her ass rise off the bed.

Kate had always been in charge when making love. Having the man take over so forcefully had her creaming all over. Who would have thought tough-as-nails Kate would like a man to dominate her? Or was it just this man?

He unfastened his trousers, his cock springing free. "Want me to stop now?"

A glance over her shoulder at his magnificent penis had her panting, "No."

His fingers trailed a path up the inside of her thighs to her warm, wet pussy, tapping into her center to drench in finger with her juices. Then he dragged his finger up to her anus and painted a circle around the tight hole before he pressed in.

Kate gasped and came up on her hands and knees, leaning back until his finger was completely inside her asshole. "Yes! That hurts so good."

He leaned over her back, his other hand massaging her breast. "Better than you could have wished?"

"Oh, yes!"

Will climbed up on the bed behind her and touched the tip of his penis against her pussy. "Want all of me?"

"Yes, oh yes," she sobbed.

With his hands planted firmly on her hips, he slid into her, his cock filling her all the way down to his balls.

Her channel stretched to accommodate his length and girth and she practically purred at the way he felt inside her. Balancing on one hand, she flicked her clit in rhythm with his thrusts, tension building to a screaming pitch.

He pumped in and out of her, slamming against her with such force the bed shook with each stroke.

When her pleasure reached a ragged peak, she plunged over the edge, her body pulsing with her orgasm. Her arms buckled beneath her until her face hit the sheets, her ass still high in the air.

Will rocked like a piston into her several more times. Then he buried himself in her cunt and held her snug against him as he shot his seed deep inside her channel.

"Damn good thing I'm on the Pill," Kate said, her voice muffled by the sheets. "I could get used to this real quick." She eased her way down on the bed until she lay flat, Will coming down with her, pressing her into the mattress.

Breathless from the hard sex and the man spread out over her, Kate couldn't help the smile curving her lips. "Wow."

"That's what they all say," Will said, kissed the back of her neck. He withdrew his cock and leaped off the bed before Kate could flip over and take aim.

"What a rotten thing to say after…after…ah, fuck!" She jumped to her feet, her knees giving way as soon as she stood. Damn. She'd thought she was in better shape than that. Why was she all the sudden as limp as a noodle? "What did you do to me?" she said, grasping his arm to catch herself before she fell.

Blond brows rose high on his forehead. "I'd say you've been thoroughly fucked."

"No shit."

"And without any wishes."

The man was infuriating to rub it in. "Okay, you made your point."

"So do I have your promise?"

Her lips twisted and she thought of all she could be missing out on if she agreed to his demand. He was asking a lot of her. But if she wanted his help... "Okay, okay. I promise not to wish you to fuck me like a whore."

Will's brows knitted. "Why do I feel like that wasn't a very sincere promise?"

She held her hand behind her back, her fingers crossed. "It was exactly what you asked me to promise, wasn't it?"

"Yes, but—"

"Then come on. We have to find the Eye." She dashed back into the living room and threw on her clothes.

Will dressed more slowly, a satisfied grin tilting his lips.

When he was done, Kate grabbed his hand, remembering the feel of them between her legs. She almost ditched the idea of finding the Eye to go for another round of monkey sex with Will. But she was so close to finding her father and the strength in Will's fingers made her feel like they could accomplish anything together.

"And how do you plan to do find the Eye?" he asked.

"By wishing, of course." She closed her eyes, feeling closer to her destination than she ever had. "I wish Will and I were in the same place as the Eye of the Serpent."

Will groaned, his gaze cast heavenward. "I hope the Eye is not in Hell."

* * * * *

Harry opened his eyes and stared around the cool interior of a plush hotel room. "Where are we?" Then he remembered the shooting and he spun around. He and Edie were alone. "Are you all right?"

"I'm fine," she said. "What about you?"

"Not a scratch." Harry walked through an open doorway. "Anybody here?"

No response. He returned to the sitting room, a puzzled frown on his face. "What exactly did you wish for?"

"I wished we were in the same place as Will."

"He's not here."

"I can see that. I don't understand." She wandered around the room, toed a loose towel on the floor and stared out the window. "Any idea where we are?"

He came to stand beside her at the window staring out at the foreign landscape of white buildings, baking in desert heat. "No idea."

"I wished it right. Why isn't Will here?"

"Well, we know your wishes have a tendency to backfire."

"Not that much." She turned to inspect the room again, her gaze scanning every item. Edie gasped and raced for the couch. "Harry, look at this." She turned and held a bottle in the air. One that looked very much like the bottle Harry had come from. That bottle was safely stashed in a burned-out hull of a house in some obscure desert town in Iraq, along with the Stone of Azhi. Hopefully, no one had found it.

"You think Will might have been in this?" Harry asked.

"Had to be." Edie's eyes lit with excitement. "Will was here!"

Harry pulled the cushions off the couch and strode back into the bedroom and bathroom. "That's the only bottle in the room. I wonder where Mitch is?"

"I don't know, but I'd guess Will has only recently discovered what happened. We need to find him and the woman who freed him before something terrible happens."

"Yeah, we do." He kissed the tip of Edie's nose, then her lips.

She sighed and kissed him back.

God, he loved this woman who had the outward appearance of a museum matron and the heart of an adventurer. "Want to do the honors or shall we stay here and make love?"

"Ummm, tough decision." Her arms snaked around his neck and she slid a leg up the side of his, rubbing her cunt against his thigh.

Harry was completely lost in the arms of the woman he loved when the hotel door crashed in.

Two monstrous men charged in with guns aimed at Harry and Edie.

"Do the honors, Edie, quick," he muttered against her hair.

Even more frightening than the two boys packing heat was the woman who followed them.

"Didn't she get enough back in New York City?" Harry asked.

Danorah Hakala, the sleek blonde terror who'd tried to kill them less than a week ago, stepped through the door.

"Give me the Stone of Azhi and I will let you live," she said in a heavily accented voice.

"And if I don't?" Harry asked.

Edie moved into Harry's arms. "Harry, I'm so scared. Please, don't argue with the woman, give her what she wants." She pressed close to Harry and whispered into his chest, "Oh, baby, I wish we were where Will is."

* * * * *

Once he got his feet under him, Will patted himself down to make sure nothing was on fire or smoking. When he was satisfied his body wasn't in any immediate danger, he studied their palatial surroundings. "This place looks like the Taj Mahal. I believe you might have gotten it right this time, Kate."

The woman he'd met only an hour ago was already walking away. When she reached a corner she stopped and peered around. Less than a second later, she ducked back and pressed a finger to her lips, her eyes wide.

Will hurried toward her. "What is it?"

"I hear someone coming."

He peered over her shoulder but couldn't see anything. "Perhaps we can ask these people where exactly we are."

She eased her head around the corner again and popped back immediately. "Uh, I don't think that's a good idea."

"Why not?"

"There's three of them and one of the three isn't coming willingly. Hide!" Kate ran across the marble floors and back down the wide hallway lined with Roman columns.

A man cried out from around the corner, his cries turning into a pleading wail.

Will raced after Kate as she ducked into an arched alcove and hid behind a potted palm the size of a giraffe.

Soon the two men Kate spoke of marched by, wearing the white garb of an Arab with a black-and-white *kaffiyeh* headdress secured by a red braided *Igal*. A man stumbled between them, as they dragged him down the hall. He shook his head, his eyes streaming with tears.

Will recognized a few words of Farsi.

"What is he saying?" Kate whispered.

"Something about stealing and that he didn't do it." Will strained to translate the words between the man's sobbing and wailing.

"Do you think they'll kill him?" she asked.

"I don't know."

The men disappeared around another corner.

"Come on." Kate took off after the men.

"Where are you going?" His gut was telling him they should be running the opposite direction, but Kate didn't wait for him. She was halfway down the hall before he caught up.

"I want to make sure they don't kill that man."

"And how do you propose to stop them? There are two of them." Was this woman insane? If they weren't careful, they might end up like the unfortunate man being dragged away. Will was beginning to regret agreeing to assist Kate in her plan.

"And there are two of us." She stopped and turned toward him. "Are you going to argue with me about everything?"

"As far as I'm concerned, this isn't an argument and following those men is not part of our agreement."

"Fine. I'll take care of them myself." Kate tossed her long black hair over her shoulder and hurried away.

I'm not going after her. She deserves whatever she gets. Will paced back and forth across the width of the spacious hall.

Kate stopped at the corner and waved him on.

Will crossed his arms over his chest and shook his head, mouthing the word "No".

"Don't make me wish it, Will," she said in a loud whisper.

Damn the woman. "You wouldn't."

"Don't try me."

Will moved toward her despite his better judgment. "Is there ever a time you don't have to argue, threaten or wish a man to do what you want?"

"Until you, I've never had a problem. Now shut up and let's get moving before we lose them." Kate took off running down another wide hallway.

Will ran after her. When he reached the next corner, the tinny music of the Middle East could be clearly heard. An ornate latticework wall stood between them and a room that appeared to be full of people.

Kate dropped to a crouch and inched toward the lattice.

"What are you doing?" Will asked.

"Checking it out. Shhh!"

Will crept up beside her, peering through he tightly scrolled curves of wood.

Two dozen men sat on ornate pillows with their backs to Will and Kate. Others were scattered around the room, not a part of the semicircle, and their pillows weren't as elaborately embroidered as the main guests. All the men faced the center of the room, where the man they'd seen dragged down the hallway kneeled. He sobbed into his hands and bowed low to kiss the ground. The two guards stood on either side of the man, their arms crossed over their chests.

The robed man at the center of the semicircle raised his hand and spoke something in Farsi.

Will only caught every other word.

"The important-looking man speaking is Sheik Sayyid. Apparently, this is his palace. The distraught man is accused of stealing from the sheik," Will translated for Kate.

"What did he steal?" Kate asked.

"If I'm not mistaken, food."

"Poor man."

The sheik spoke again. Will concentrated on his words, his mastery of the language only marginal.

"The sheik feels that if he allows a thief to get away with his crime what will he take next? His palace is full of treasures and jewels worth a lot of money."

"Jewels?" Kate glanced up, her eyes wide. "Do you think he has the Eye of the Serpent?"

"Perhaps."

Like the commander of an army about to go into battle, the sheik stood and delivered a diatribe on the evils of stealing. He emphasized his final word by pounding his fist into his palm.

Even without understanding every word, Will couldn't mistake the meaning.

"What did he say?" Kate asked.

"Nothing. Come on, we have to get out of here." He grabbed her arm and pulled.

Kate slipped free. "No. We have to help that man."

"We can't. There are more than thirty men in that room and some of them are armed."

"But we can't just stand by and watch them—"

One of the guards beside the prisoner reached down, grabbed the man's hair and yanked him to his feet.

The prisoner cried out and fought against the larger man's hold, but he didn't have a chance.

In the next second the guard sliced his throat from ear to ear.

Before Will could stop her, Kate leaped to her feet. "No!"

All heads in the room behind the lattice turned in their direction. One guest in particular caught her attention.

Kate gasped. "Qarim! That's Qarim!"

Will clamped a hand over Kate's mouth and dragged her backward. "I think it's time we left."

Several men shouted and all hell broke loose on the other side of the fancy latticework.

Will let go of her mouth and grabbed her hand, dragging her down the hallway and back the way they came. Without stopping to look back, he pulled Kate around a corner and down another shorter hall. The sound of footsteps grew closer. If they couldn't outrun the guards, they had to hide. Will ducked behind the potted palm they'd hidden behind earlier and tugged Kate in close beside him. "If you can wish us out of here, now would be a good time." He let go of her hand, bracing himself for a transfer to a less hostile environment."

"But we can't leave!" Kate said. "The Eye of the Serpent is somewhere inside this palace. It has to be." Her eyes narrowed. "I bet Qarim stole it. That weasel. That snake."

"To hell with Qarim. If you don't wish us out of here now, they'll kill us."

As if on cue, shouts erupted from both ends of the hall and they could see Arab men, robes flapping around them, racing toward their hiding place.

Will grabbed Kate's shoulders and stared down into her eyes. "Don't argue, Kate, do it!"

Her gaze locked with his, and Will held his breath. For a moment, he thought she would argue, but then she glanced over his shoulders, her eyes widening. "I wish we were someplace safe."

"That was a bit vague."

She made a face at him. "Beggars can't be choosers."

When the floors shook, the men racing toward them stumbled, the effect slowing them. Thunder echoed off the high ceilings.

Given their situation, Hell almost seemed preferable to having his throat cut. Still, if Will had a choice, somewhere away from the palace would be great. A second before his world went black, Will grabbed Kate's hand and held on. If he was going back to Hell, she could damn well come with him.

* * * * *

When the shaking and rumbling stopped, Harry opened his eyes to see green palm fronds immediately in front of his face. Edie stood beside him, blinking her eyes and bracing herself against him. All limbs were intact and his sweetheart stood beside him. Okay, so far so good.

As he became more aware of his surroundings beyond the tranquil little oasis behind the tree, he noticed the phalanx of Arab soldiers with some kind of assault weapons pointed at Edie and him.

"Harry? Where's Will? I know I wished us to where Will was."

Harry stood as still as a stone in a graveyard, answering her between clenched teeth. "He's not here."

Edie rubbed her eyes and stared through the tree. With a gasp, she clutched his arm and pointed at the soldiers. "Why are those men pointing guns at us?"

"I don't know, honey, why don't you ask them?"

Chapter Five

&

Kate staggered as she "landed", glad for the hand in hers to steady her.

Will's hand.

How had she come to rely so heavily on him in such a short time? She didn't even know the man? Yet, after a year of searching on her own, having Will with her was so much better. She could share her difficulties, frustrations and ideas with him. Although he argued too much with her, she could put up with a lot just for the company. Not to mention the great sex.

She already regretted her promise. She'd like nothing better than to have more raunchy sex with this man. How handy to get great sex any time you wished.

"Where are we?" Will asked.

His question broke into Kate's short journey into self-indulgent thoughts. "I don't know."

The room was light and airy, with pastel-colored pillows and pallets strewn around the room.

"This looks very feminine. A woman or women must live here," Kate said.

"Women?" Will's stomach knotted. "Like a harem?"

Kate's eyes widened. "Perhaps."

"Then we better get out of here. Do sheiks kill intruders who dare to set foot in their private harems?"

"I don't know. But there's no one here right now, so I think we're safe for the moment."

"I think it's too soon to feel safe after what they did to that guy back there."

Kate shivered. She'd never witnessed such blatant cruelty and hoped never to witness it again. "We have to find the Eye of the Serpent before we can leave this palace."

"And you think it might be in the harem?"

"No. But the wish took us where we'd be safe, so have a little faith."

"As long as the women are not in here surrounded by whatever contingent of guards." Will wrapped an arm around her waist and pulled her against him. "Are you all right?"

"Yeah." Her heart fluttered in her chest and pussy tingled. If he knew what she'd been thinking a few moments earlier, he wouldn't feel so safe, would he? "Now to find out where they've taken the Eye."

"By the way, who is Qarim?" Will asked.

"He's a man who deals in the black market—a jerk and a thief. That bastard stole the Eye of the Serpent. I just know it." Kate paced across the room and back. "That has to be why he's here. He's going to sell it to Sheik Sayyid, if he hasn't already." She stopped and stared hard at the floor. "Bastard."

A giggle sounded behind them.

Will glanced over her shoulder and a smile spread across his face. "Kate, you did it. You landed us in Heaven."

Kate spun toward a group of women standing in an open arched doorway. "Question is will your angels turn us in? Turn up the wattage, Romeo."

His grin faded. "Huh?"

She rolled her eyes. "Give them one of your killer smiles, Will."

With raised brows, he glanced at her. "And I was beginning to wonder if you ever noticed." He winked.

"Just do it, damn it," she said through gritted teeth.

Will turned to the group of women and smiled, full shine. His light, sandy blond hair, blue eyes and sexy smile were perhaps their best weapon against this mob of lovely ladies.

The women were beautifully dressed in belly-dancing clothing with the bright gold bangle belts, gauzy leg coverings and sequined bras.

A collective sigh went up among them and they all rushed forward at once, the combined chiming a cacophony of music.

"Look out, we're about to be surrounded." Will backed against a pillow-like sleeping pallet and fell, landing amid sheets of red, gold and purple satin.

Women sank down onto the pallet with him and stroked him from head to foot.

Will tucked his hands behind his head and sighed. "I think I'm going to like this."

Kate stood tapping her toe, a snarl on her face. "Don't get too comfortable. We have to find the Eye. Does anyone speak English here?"

All faces turned to her and their voices rose as one. "We do."

With a laugh, Kate propped a hand on her hip. "Do all Arabic women learn English?"

An auburn-haired woman rolled her blue-sequined breast off Will and cocked her head to the side. "A lot of the Arabic women speak English, but none of us are from Saudi." She pressed a kiss to Will's lips and pushed back to her feet. Several other women stood as well.

Kate stuck out a hand. "I'm Kate Ralston from California in America. And you are?"

"Haley Jones. Rochester, New York."

"Moira O'Malley, Dublin." A strawberry blonde smiled as she leaned over Will. "And you are…?"

"Enchanted." Will sighed, much to Kate's ire. "William Moreland, but you can call me Will."

One after one the women introduced themselves as either from Europe or America.

A confused frown settled between Kate's brows. "Why are you here? Are you prisoners?"

"Oh, no, not at all," Haley said. "We're all dancers for Sheik Sayyid. This was the best gig for the money."

"Dancers?" Will clapped his hands from his reclined position on the pillowed pallet. "Kate, you really did land me in Heaven this time."

Haley shook her head, causing the little gold bells sewn into the turquoise-blue chiffon to jingle. "I wouldn't quite call it Heaven. We're under close watch and the guards are usually right on top of us. But they're all combing the other side of the palace for intruders, as we speak." Her eyes widened as the words left her mouth. "You?"

Kate nodded. "I'm afraid they're looking for us."

"Why? Did you kill someone or something?"

"No, but we saw them kill a man for stealing food."

Haley's face paled. "Holy shit! No kidding?"

"Who?" Moira asked.

"I don't know. Is Sheik Sayyid the owner of this palace?"

"Yeah." Haley waved her hand around the room. "He owns this palace and two others. The man has about a hundred or more oil wells and more money than God."

Moira shook her head. "I'd heard he was ruthless, but I didn't realize he would murder a man in public."

"Well, he did and now he's after us." Will climbed to his feet, the ladies following his lead.

Haley stroked her chin, her heavily lined eyes narrowing into two dark slits. "We can hide Kate by saying she's one of us, but we may have a problem hiding Will."

Moira looked back at Will, her mouth curving into a wicked smile. "I don't know. He is rather pretty for a man."

Will squared his shoulders, a scowl forming on his forehead. "Men aren't pretty."

Kate could tell he was uncomfortable under Moira's speculative gaze. He puffed out his chest, trying to look manlier than he already was. The guy practically oozed testosterone. When he reached up to push his blond hair back, Kate knew he was nervous.

With a speculative gleam, Haley considered Will. "You know, with the right scarves and jewelry..."

"Oh no you're not." He held up his hands and backed away from the women.

"Come on, Will. We might learn something by going undercover," Kate said.

A brunette standing close to the doorway hissed, "Hey! We got company coming."

All eyes turned to Will, Kate's included. If they didn't hide him quickly, he might meet the same fate as the food thief.

* * * * *

"Why the woman gets the wishes, I'll never understand," Harry lamented as he pulled off his boots and dropped his pants.

"Like you would have done better?" Edie said from across the room, tugging her shirt over her head. She stood in nothing but her bra and panties, her deep red hair curling softly around her shoulders and her color high in her cheeks.

Harry was amazed this woman could still blush after the sexual antics they'd performed. "I'm still flabbergasted at how you convinced Sheik Sayyid we should be treated as guests and not have out heads lopped off."

"I think my mention of the archeological dig in the Zagros Mountains of Iraq caught his interest. But when the subject came up about the Devil King's daughter, Princess Vashti, he was hooked."

He strode across the room and pulled her into his arms. "You were brilliant asking him for additional funding to continue our work."

Edie laid her cheek against his bare chest. "We must be careful not to tell him anything about the Stone of Azhi."

"Right, Danorah is annoying enough without having Sayyid's thugs chasing us with guns." Harry loved the feel of her warm skin against his.

"I'm just glad he didn't slice our throats." A tremor rippled across her body.

"Me too." He kissed the top of her head and squeezed her tighter, his growing erection pressing against her belly. "The fewer people who know about the stone, the better."

"Exactly." She smiled crookedly. "At least we got a room without bars and we're about to get a fabulous bath, if the pool behind the curtain is any indication."

"Pool?" Harry's body tingled at the thought of getting into a pool with the lovely Edie. "Have you ever made love in a pool, Edie?"

"You know I haven't. You're my first lover." She sighed. "You are so much more experienced than I am. I wish—"

Harry's heart leaped in his chest and he slammed his mouth over hers. He slipped his hands down to her ass to pull her tight against him. With his cock pulsing against her soft skin, he rocked his hips as an invitation to join him in a little exercise. When he broke the kiss, he lifted a finger to her lips. "You wish nothing. Say it, Edie." Harry held his breath, waiting for her words.

"Nothing." She sighed. "I wish for nothing."

Releasing the breath from his lungs, Harry relaxed. "Sorry, sweetheart. But sometimes you scare me."

Edie frowned for a moment then leaned into him and kissed him full on the mouth. "It's a good thing I love you, Harry. I'd even lie for you." She tipped her head to the side. "I'm actually getting quite good at it."

"Do you think they really bought all that hogwash?" Harry asked.

"I don't know, but if they didn't you can bet that we're being watched." Edie pushed away from him and padded around the room checking light fixtures, potted plants and furniture.

"What are you looking for?" Harry asked.

"Bugs." She ducked down and looked at the underside of a table and chair set.

"We are on a potentially deadly mission and you're worried about bugs?" Edie did strange things every now and then. Harry was beginning to think the twenty-first century was one very odd place to be compared to the relative simplicity of his world in 1924.

"I'm sorry, Harry. Sometimes I forget you aren't familiar with our time. A bug is a small radio transmitter. I'm also looking for miniature cameras they might have positioned at various points in the room to watch our every move."

Harry moved in behind her, his arms circling her naked waist. "Does it bother you that they might be watching?"

Edie leaned against him, rubbing her bottom over his cock. "Mmm. Did you say something about bothered? Because, yes, I'm very bothered."

"That's right, let's give them a show they won't forget." He swung her up in his arms and marched around the curtain to the bathing area.

"I love it when you act like a caveman." Edie nuzzled his neck and reached up to bite his earlobe.

The pool was the size of the living room in Edie's small apartment back in New York City. And the water looked clean and refreshing after the hot, dry desert they'd been stuck in for the past few days.

"I probably smell like a caveman." Harry couldn't wait to clean the grime from his body and from hers. The thought of rubbing soap over her breasts and cunt nearly made him come.

Edie pressed her nose to his chest and sniffed. She blinked her eyes and smiled. "Yup, you do smell like a caveman."

Without warning, Harry dropped Edie to her feet. In two easy movements, he had her bra off and her panties slung across the room. "Come, woman. I want to make love to you and I can't until I'm clean." He slung her over his shoulder in a fireman's carry.

Edie squealed and halfheartedly pounded against his back. "Put me down. I can walk."

"No, as a caveman I have to show you who's the boss." He marched down the shallow steps into the pool until he was waist deep. Then he flipped her over and into the water, going in after her.

They surfaced laughing and sputtering. Coming together in each other's arms.

Edie grabbed a bar of scented soap from the side of the pool and lathered it in her hands. "Umm. Smells like jasmine. How to you feel about smelling like a flower, Harry?"

"If you promise to rub that all over me, I don't care if I smell like a rose."

She slathered the foam over his chest, lacing her fingers through the curly hairs, following them downward into the water. Her hands wrapped around his penis, the slippery soap dissolving in warm water.

Slender fingers traced the hard line of him to the swollen end, circling the velvety smooth tip.

Harry dropped his head back and groaned. "If they have cameras on us, they will get to see a lot more than skin."

"Harry?" Her hands stopped their tender torment and she looked up at him.

"Yes, Edie?" Harry said through clenched teeth. Did she not know what she was doing to him?

"Are we selfish to enjoy this...bath so much when our friends might be in trouble?"

"I'm sure Will and Mitch would forgive us if they knew the situation. Please, Edie, don't stop."

"Oh." Her eyes widened. "You like that?"

"Sometimes, Edie, I wonder if you are really so naïve or if it's all an act." He pulled her roughly against him and kissed her soundly on the lips. Then he hiked her bottom up on the edge of the pool. "Let me demonstrate to you what it feels like."

"But Harry, I wanted to do you."

"Later." He knelt down in the pool, the water lapping up to his shoulders, his mouth achingly close to her pussy. "I want to pleasure my cavewoman."

"I guess Will and Mitch can take care of themselves for a moment. I'm feeling very dirty." Edie's mouth curved into a sexy smile and she opened her legs wide. "I'm liking this bath more and more by the minute."

Harry's chest tightened at Edie's adventurous spirit. He really had found a woman who could match him in bed and out and she fired his soul. Not to mention a few other physical points. Trailing a long string of kisses leading from her inner knee to the soft mound of red curls, Harry finally arrived at the place he liked most. His tongue dove into the warm, moist entrance of her cunt, lapping at her musky juices.

Edie's back arched and her hands slid up to cup her breasts. "Harry. That feels sooo good."

"If you think that feels good, let me show you even better."

"I don't know, Harry." She laced her hands in his hair, stroking it back from his forehead. "It would have to be pretty sensational to top this."

Harry tongued her entrance once more, smiled and kissed her thigh. "Watch me." With a glance upward to see that she was looking, he traced a path with his tongue from her pussy upward. Parting her folds with his fingers, he flicked her clit with the tip of a finger.

Edie's legs tightened around him. "Close. The feeling is really close. But no cigar." She smiled a knowing grin with a raised eyebrow.

"Did I say I was through?" He nipped at her inner thigh.

"Do you need help determining where to go?"

"Perhaps."

"Just like a man to resist asking for directions." She sighed an exaggerated huff. "Pay attention. I'm only going to show you once."

Oh, he paid attention all right.

Her hands started at her breasts, tweaking the nipples into hardened peaks and then inched their way down over her ribs. With her index finger, she swirled around then dipped into her bellybutton.

Harry panted, wanting his tongue to be dipping there. "And to think you were a virgin less than two weeks ago." Two weeks ago when she'd woken him from a bottle after sleeping for eighty years. Two weeks since she'd found him and he'd fallen in love with the sensitive woman with the spirit of a warrior.

"I'm a quick learner," she said.

"Oh, yes." He stretched up and took one of her fingers into his mouth, sucking on it.

Edie frowned and pulled it back, tapping the tip of his nose with the damp digit. "Patience. You're not there yet."

"I'm so close I could taste it."

She just smiled and laid her finger back on her belly, splaying both hands wide. Pushing downward, she laced in and out of the curly red hairs covering her mons. "Are you getting this?"

Harry moaned and pressed his eyelids shut. Getting it? Oh yes, he was getting it so badly, his head spun. Afraid he'd miss more of her brazen display, he opened his eyes.

Her fingers parted her folds and slipped in to stroke her clit.

Mouth watering, Harry could take it no longer. "I have to have you. Now."

Edie laughed out loud as Harry dove in and sucked her clit into his mouth, pulling hard enough to make her cry out. "Easy, boy. Easy."

Vowing to make up for his lack of control, he laved her clit slowly, gently until Edie lay back with a sigh against the tile floor, draping her legs over his shoulders. His fingers worked their own magic on her pussy, circling the entrance, painting her opening with her own juices. Then he traced a digit downward to her anus, poking into the tight little hole.

Edie gasped and bucked beneath him.

"It's okay." He smoothed another finger of lubrication down to the puckered lips of her asshole and pushed in again.

Her thighs tightened around his shoulders, warming his ears.

"Relax." He blew a cool stream of air over her moistened pussy and anus and then pushed a finger deeper into her ass. At the same time, he licked her clit, alternating between long, flat slurps and tiny flickers.

Her body tensed and just as Edie plunged over the edge of orgasm, Harry stopped.

With a moan of protest, Edie reached out. "Don't stop now!"

"I couldn't if I wanted to." Harry stood, steam rising from his hot, hard cock. He hooked her legs over his arms and pulled her closer to the edge of the pool. Then he slammed into her cunt hard and fast, fucking her so hard, his balls made slapping sounds against her ass. Harder, faster, he pumped, his body tensing until he burst into a thousand pieces, falling, falling, falling back to earth, into his merely mortal body.

Harry lay over Edie on the edge of the pool, her warm body cushioning his from the cold hard tile. Nuzzling her neck he whispered into her hair, "Just think…it's even better in the water."

She nibbled his ear. "Prove it."

Spent but not without reserve strength where loving Edie was concerned, Harry summoned enough energy to toss her into the water and go in after her. Half an hour later, when they both came up for air, Edie leaned against Harry's chest.

"Do you think Will and Mitch will forgive us that?" she asked, twirling a strand of hair around her finger.

Harry smoothed her wet hair from her face and kissed her temple. "I guarantee it."

"Then let's go find them and ask."

Chapter Six

** හ**

"No, I won't do it!" Will dug his bare feet into the tiles and leaned against the half-dozen female hands propelling him forward.

"Will, you have to," Kate insisted. "It's either go out and dance or explain to the guards behind us why you refuse."

"I'll tell them I'm shy. Hell, Kate, I'd rather face a room full of guards than be seen in public dressed like a harem girl. If Harry saw me in this, he'd never let me live it down."

"Harry's not here and you don't know anyone out there, not that they'd recognize you. Now don't insult the other dancers' clothing and get over your modesty." Kate stepped away from him and peeked through the rich red drapes separating the dancers from the audience of men awaiting the entertainment.

Music started in the reedy notes of instruments Will had heard before when he and Harry had been wined and dined by the sheik of a small town in Iraq back in 1924. A very long time ago, yet the memory was fresh in Will's mind. "We're supposed to be finding Harry, not dancing."

"We will," she said without turning. "Just as soon as I get the Eye of the Serpent."

"And how is dancing for a group of lecherous men supposed to help?"

"It keeps us undiscovered for a little longer and I'm hoping to slip away while the men and guards' attention is on the dancing."

"And they won't think it odd to have an overly tall woman with hairy legs cavorting in front of them?"

Kate stared down at Will's legs completely covered in long silk scarves of red, gold and green. Similar veils were used to drape along his torso, wrists and head. With his light blue eyes shining through the dark eyeliner and mascara, he looked like a female. Unfortunately he didn't walk or talk like a female. "Do the best you can to keep the hair under the scarves. And for Pete's sake, swing your hips more."

"I'm a man, not a woman. I don't have the knowledge or equipment to swing my hips."

"Watch the other girls." Kate waved at the women standing around smiling at Will. Several rocked their hips and their gold belts trimmed with what looked like miniature coins jangled. At any other time, Will would enjoy the display. Faced with having to perform such complicated movements, he was not at all appreciative of their efforts.

"Practice a little." Kate tapped his hip. "It's not that hard. Watch." She swung her hips in a slow side-to-side motion. "It's all a figure eight pattern."

Where the other women weren't that interesting, Kate's hips moving suggestively made his cock twitch. He grabbed those gyrating hips and held them still. Then with a deep breath he spoke to her in the tones of a father lecturing an especially hardheaded child. "Kate, you don't get it. I'm a man. Watching you is only going to make matters worse. Besides, men don't do this."

"Well, you better, because we're on in ten minutes."

That sinking feeling attacked Will's gut. How he got himself into situations like this he didn't know. But the first opportunity he found, he was out of here and back on the trail of finding Harry. Kate could figure out her own problems. Huh! Make a man dress like a woman. Huh!

Moira hurried over and caught Will's arm. "Hey, I overheard one of the guards saying they caught the man and the woman sneaking around the palace."

"What?" Will dropped into a ready-stance and surveyed all entrances leading into the area where they waited.

"How can that be?" Kate asked. "We're here."

"Not you two, silly." She glanced back at the guard standing by the door. "Someone else. But instead of holding them captive, they're going to be guests at this dinner."

"Are they serving them as the main course?" Will asked.

"Don't be maudlin!" Kate made a face and slapped at Will's arm, but her face was pale. No doubt remembering the earlier scene with the throat slashing.

"No, they said something about buried treasure and Sheik Sayyid got excited."

"Interesting." He could understand the excitement of buried treasure. Wasn't that what he and Harry had been after when this whole mess started? Will strode to the curtain and peeked through. The guests were beginning to arrive and servants scurried around straightening pillows and setting out goblets. A group of musicians sat in a corner, playing their instruments softly.

"Great. I was hoping to sneak out before they arrived," Will muttered.

Kate stepped up beside him and adjusted a veil. "You'll be just fine. If it helps, you look absolutely beautiful." She stared into his eyes and smiled. "Especially your baby-blues."

Will wanted to pull Kate into his arm, but the silky fabric felt too feminine and…and wrong. He couldn't wait to strip naked and take this woman again. On his own terms and not wearing paint on his face.

One last peek at the crowd settling into their chairs and Will's stomach filled with dread. He turned away and walked toward the guards. "I can't do this."

Kate hurried alongside him, skipping to keep up. "You have to. These guards will not let you out at this point." As if to emphasize her point, the guards' chests swelled making them look even bigger than they already were. They moved together completely blocking the door with their muscular bulk.

"I can take them on," Will said beneath his breath, but his footsteps slowed.

"Just get through this dance and we'll be back in the room, the guards won't be watching and we can get away—no one the wiser and no one will question your masculinity." She squeezed his arm and her voice dropped into a slow sexy purr. "Especially not me."

His ego somewhat assuaged, Will stood in the middle of the floor, studying his adversaries. The two men guarding the door, the room full of women preparing to dance and one black-haired, blue-eyed witch with a penchant for leading him on wild goose chases with unexpected detours.

Will stared down into the witch's eyes and knew he couldn't disappoint her. Hell, she'd probably put a curse on him or something. Most likely she already had. He could feel himself falling under her spell from the moment he first saw her in that white towel and those long, creamy legs.

"All right. But we get the Eye and get out of this palace as soon as possible."

"Right." She leaned up and kissed him on the cheek.

"Hey!" He glanced at the two guards watching them with interest. "What are those guards going to think?"

She shrugged. "That we are lesbians. What else?" With that parting shot, she flounced away.

"Masculinity intact, my ass."

The music chimed louder and Haley turned to the other women. "That's our cue, girls. We're on!" She held the curtain back as the others filed through. "Don't worry, Will, just follow our lead." Kate held the curtain for her and she stepped out her hips swaying, bangles jingling.

"I can't do this," Will said, staring into the room full of men openly leering at the dancers as they cavorted around the room in time to the music.

"Of course you can." She moved behind him and shoved him past the curtain and out into the open room.

If Kate weren't a woman, Will would have slugged her. But she was a woman. And the way she was shaking her hips... What did he do to deserve this situation?

Touched a stone in a tomb. That's what. He had to find Harry and undo the damage. But for now, his life depended on him blending in with a bunch of female dancers. With a tentative move, he hiked one hip up then the other. The belt and bangles draped around his body rang merrily.

Okay, so this wasn't so hard. He did it again and added a step to propel him forward around the room like the other girls. Figure eights, that's what Kate said. Nothing to it but one figure eight after another. The more he moved the easier it got. With an eye on Sheik Sayyid and the group sitting at the end of the room, Qarim included, Will twirled around the room, looking for all the exits.

The whole time he danced, he reminded himself no one knew him here. None of this would ever get back to the guys in the bars in Chicago.

Wait. Will stopped for a moment, considering the direction of his thoughts. Those guys were dead by now. Any friend he had was either over one hundred years old or dead. How depressing to think he didn't really know anyone in this century except Kate. His only friend who might not be dead was the man who'd gotten him into this mess in the first place.

Harry.

At that moment, a red-haired woman escorted by a guard entered the room behind the sheik. She was followed by a man with dark hair and brown eyes. A man who looked surprisingly like Harry!

In his excitement, Will almost forgot where he was and charged forward, a grin spreading across his face. Before he got three yards, Kate stepped in front of him and whirled, clicking miniature cymbals together on her fingertips. "I found a way out," she whispered.

"Huh?"

"Out? Escape? Will, stay with me, boy." She smiled. "You really are getting into this dance, aren't you?" She whirled away, her body flowing to the music. At least a dozen men stared at her naked midsection and the golden belt jangling low on her hips, probably wondering if it would fall along with the sequined panties.

No women he knew back in the Twenties would wear such an outfit. Okay, so maybe the ladies of the evening he frequented back in Chicago. The problem was that Will knew what was under that little scrap of fabric. Growing hot all over, he turned away from those swaying hips, determined not to expose himself by getting hard while in women's clothing.

Impersonating a female dancer might be high on the list for losing one's head in this palace. And Will needed to figure out what the heck Harry was doing here as a guest.

If he could get a little closer, he might be able to ask.

Kate danced by. "I'm going to slip out and find the Eye."

"I'm coming with you," he swayed and spun after her.

"No, Will," she said, smiling and circling him. "They won't miss one dancer, but two might be more noticeable." She clicked her fingers. "I'll be back soon."

Will didn't have a good feeling about Kate's leaving. What she needed was a distraction to keep all eyes on the dancers and not the one ducking through the side doorway.

Clenching his teeth and pasting what he hoped was an alluring smile on his face, Will took the lead and swept around the semicircle of men, pausing in front of the sheik and his entourage. Imitating the movements of the other ladies, he wiggled his hips and shimmied his shoulders. Then he moved along the line of men until he stood in front of Harry.

The red-haired woman and Harry stood out in their western clothing among the Middle East garb of robes and headdresses. But he was a sight for sore eyes as far as Will was concerned—his only friend in a sea of strange faces and a world eighty years ahead of him.

Harry sat with his head tipped toward the woman, talking in low tones no one could hear over the music.

Will shook his hips and smiled directly into Harry's gaze.

The dunce's lips turned up briefly but his attention was fully captured by the woman beside him. Who was she? Harry had sworn off women the last time Will talked to him—eighty years ago.

A short round man next to Harry tossed a coin at Will and winked.

Winked! With all the control he could muster, Will danced away and back amongst the other ladies charming their audience. A quick glance around the two dozen dancers and Will knew Kate had made good her escape. Part of him wanted to disregard her warning and go after her. What if the guards captured her while she was trying to steal the Eye of the Serpent?

Swallowing the sudden lump clogging his throat, Will grew weary of dancing and discouraged he couldn't get word to Harry without alerting the sheik and all his guards. He had to try once more. Somehow he had to get to his friend and warn him of the sheik's intolerance for deception.

Will touched Haley on the arm. "Help me distract the short man next to the American."

"You lead, I'll follow." As good as her word, Haley danced across the room behind Will. When they stood in front of Sheik Sayyid and his guests, Haley went into an extraordinary belly dance including a backbend and walkover.

While the men applauded, Will shimmied over the table toward his friend and hissed in a high feminine voice, "Harry!"

Harry's head came up and he stared into Will's eyes. "Yes?" With narrowed eyes he gazed at Will as he danced. "Do I know you?"

"Yes," he said in the high voice, then dropped to his regular tone. "You do."

The little man next to Harry sat back, startled. Then he grinned and clapped his chubby hands. Before Will could step away, the man jumped up and kissed Will on the cheek.

Will leaped away, working hard not to gag or put his fist through the man's eye. He had been kissed by a man! And in front of Harry! Mortification burned in his cheeks and he turned to get away as quickly as possible.

"Stop!" The commanding voice froze Will and every other dancer on the floor. The music faded to the last off-key note.

When Will turned back to face Sheik Sayyid, he knew he'd been caught.

The man stared straight at him, his eyes narrowed, his arms crossed over his chest. For Will who avoided danger at all costs, this situation couldn't be worse. Surrounded by no less than twenty guards and as many friends of the sheik, he didn't stand a chance of bolting for safety.

So Will did what any red-blooded American male would do. He hiked his hip out, turned his head to the side and winked like a girl.

Sheik Sayyid's frowning gaze narrowed further.

For a moment, Will thought he would explode in anger.

But, much to Will's relief, the sheik's frown cleared and he burst out laughing. Then he leaned to the side and said something to the man next to him. The Arab stood and hurried across the floor to Will.

Was this the way the sheik would single him out for execution? Will stood on the balls of his feet, ready to hit the man and run toward the nearest door. He eyed the guard there sizing him up. Yeah, he might be able to take out the guard and make it out into the hallway. But how far would he get before they found him? And if they found him, would they discover Kate? Lowering himself to his flat slipper-clad feet, he waited for the sentence to be delivered.

The man wore the white robes and red-and-white *kaffiyeh* headdress of the sheik. When he stood in front of Will, he nodded his head instead of bowing. "Sheik Sayyid wishes you to perform a private dance for his honored guest Jawad." His hand swept to the side and he moved out of Will's view of the short, round man beside Harry.

Jawad wiggled his fingers and grinned.

No. He wouldn't go to the man's room and dance for him. Guys like Jawad were certain to have greater expectations than a mere dance.

Haley sidled up to Will. "If you don't go, it is considered a grave insult to the sheik and his friend. You don't have to do anything you don't want to. Just dance."

Will turned to the messenger and said in a sickly sweet and pathetic attempt at a feminine voice, "Are you sure he wants me?"

The man's gaze traveled from the satin slippers upward to his veiled head and shrugged. "Yes, it seems Jawad is taken with your dancing." The man all but rolled his eyes as if to say he couldn't see what Jawad saw in Will.

Haley nudged him in the middle of his back in silent warning to take the offer or suffer the consequences.

Will was on the verge of suffering the consequences, when Haley nudged him again.

"Okay, okay. I'll dance for Jawad," he said, not bothering to sound very feminine.

The little fat man clapped his stubby fingers together and rushed across the floor to grab Will's arm.

Will jerked his arm out of Jawad's grasp and said to the messenger, "Tell my friend, I can walk on my own."

After a few brief words to Jawad, the messenger returned to his seat beside the sheik, leaving Will to handle the little man on his own. A glance at Sheik

Sayyid confirmed the man was laughing. And what a sight he must have made.

At six feet even, Will towered over the man who appeared to be five feet tall and five feet around. The Arab had delusions of grandeur if he thought he could do it with a woman of statuesque proportions like Will. But the little man would be surprised if he tried anything. This "woman" was not tolerating any nonsense. He'd put the guy out of business if he so much as touched him.

As they walked past Harry, Will gave him a hard stare, hoping he'd understand and look for the man beneath the veils—his partner and old friend.

Harry's head was bowed to that damned redhead. But the woman was looking at him as he left the room with Jawad. Will glared at her, sure it was all her fault Harry couldn't make the connection between the woman in the seven hundred veils and his buddy.

* * * * *

Kate slipped through the hallways, ducking guards and hiding behind potted plants and curtains whenever necessary. Working under the assumption the sheik would live in the most opulent portion of the palace, she moved from one room to the next searching for richer furnishings and locked or heavily guarded doors. The sheik kept a vast collection, if it was all the dancers had made it out to be. A collection that large and expensive had to be well protected.

In her gut, Kate knew Qarim had stolen the Eye and sold it to Sayyid. She just had to find it and get the hell out of the palace before they discovered it missing.

What about Will? Was he still dancing with the other women? Her heart jumped into her throat. Or had they discovered his deception and slit his throat?

Panic snaked through her body like a loose electrical wire. No. Will had to be okay. Kate slowed in her search and reflected on the man who'd been an argumentative thorn in her side since she began her day. Although she had to admit, she liked that he stood up to her. And boy did their arguments make her hot. There also was his ability to grant her wishes, which had helped her out of several tight situations. Coming to an abrupt halt, she could have smacked her forehead with her own palm.

Wishes! Why the hell was she searching through the hallways when she could wish herself there in the blink of an eye? And then she could wish Will to join her when the coast was clear. "I wish I were in the room with the Eye of the Serpent."

As the marble floors beneath her shook and thunder echoed off the high ceilings, doubt crept in. Had she just made a huge mistake? Was she on her own trip to Hell? If only Will were with her this time. As her world went black, Kate braced herself for what might come.

* * * * *

"Did you see the way that dancer glared at me?" Edie asked Harry.

"What dancer?" Harry nuzzled her neck and thought of a dozen places he'd rather be with a naked Edie beneath him. At least by kissing her and playing with her hair, he could keep the sheik and his cronies from thinking they were there to spy on them. Which of course was exactly what they were up to.

Edie tipped her head to the side to allow him more access to her throat. "The one that leaned close to you earlier and called your name."

"She did?" Harry glanced into the sea of bright colored skirts and jeweled tops for the really tall one with the manly build and the abundance of scarves from head to toe. "The gangly one who was dancing in front of us? She danced more like a man." He leaned forward again and nibbled her earlobe. "I was busy trying to eavesdrop on the conversations around us. I'd hoped to find out if they had captured Will or Mitch. Fortunately, I was distracted by a beautiful woman."

"Pay attention, Harry." Edie planted a hand on either side of his face and made him look directly into her eyes. "That tall one, who is leaving as we speak, said she knew you."

Harry twisted in his seat to watch the lanky woman leaving the room in a wave of flamboyant scarves. "I swear, I've never seen her before in my life."

The woman turned back once more, a desperate look in her eyes. Eyes the same color as his friend Will's.

"She's not very feminine, is she?" The last word left his mouth as comprehension hit him like a brick to the forehead. "Damn."

Chapter Seven

 споряд

With Jawad bringing up the rear, Will followed the guard to an opulent suite several twists and turns away from the entertainment room and Harry. The farther they went, the more frustrated Will grew. How was he going to get out of this little exhibition without killing someone or alerting the guards? He had to find Harry and Kate and get the hell out of this nightmare of deception, wishes and magical stones.

The fact that the guards hadn't been summoned to a chase made him a little less apprehensive for Kate. But the thought of dancing one-on-one for a leering old codger did nothing to ease the knot in Will's belly.

Once inside Jawad's quarters, Will moved around the room searching for a way to escape without going past the guard waiting outside the door.

As soon as the door closed behind the guard, Jawad held out his arms. "Come to me, my sweet," he said in heavily accented English. With a smile of anticipation spread across his pudgy face, he waited for Will to comply.

As far as Will was concerned, the man could wait until Hell froze over. He touched a finger to his brow in remembrance of the scorching heat. "Didn't you want me to dance?" he said, sidling out of the man's reach. Not that he wanted to dance, but he certainly wasn't going along with the other delusional ideas the short Arab might have.

He shook his head. "No, you dance for me later. I want you now."

Falling back on Haley's advice, Will lifted his hands to his veil-covered cheeks. "Sir! I am not that kind of girl. I am a respectable dancer." Surely, this man didn't think every dancing girl was out to make an extra buck by sleeping with the audience?

Jawad frowned. "You do not want Jawad, you know, to fuck?"

The mere thought of this man poking his penis into any dancer made Will's stomach roil. *Especially since Jawad had his eye on yours truly.* How was Will supposed to extricate himself from this situation without raising an alarm? What he wouldn't give to have Kate's ability to wish himself out of there.

"If pretty lady not come to Jawad, Jawad come to pretty lady." The little round man moved quicker than Will expected and had him in a bear hug around the middle before Will could react.

With his arms around Will's waist, Jawad was eye-level with Will's chest. The man buried his face in the veils, nuzzling his nose through the silken fabric until he reached skin. Hair-covered skin.

"Huh?" With his arms still locked around Will, Jawad leaned back and looked up into Will's eyes. "What is this? Perhaps American girls have more hair in places our women do not?"

With a smile hidden beneath the veil, Will shook his head. He'd been found out by a very dimwitted man. "No. American women are built very much the same as Arabian women."

Jawad dropped his hands from around Will's waist. "I do not understand."

With one hand on the veil over his face, Will said, "I'm sorry to disappoint you, but I'm not a woman. I'm a man." With a quick tug, the veil fell away from his face, exposing his mouth and chin. "Now do you understand?"

The frown Jawad leveled at Will cleared, replaced by a wide grin. "You are a man?"

"Yes." Whew. He felt better already just shedding the stupid veil over his face.

"Good. Jawad like the men even better than the big women. You will fuck with Jawad? Yes?"

Will fought the bile rising in his throat. The man liked to…to… Will couldn't bring himself to think of such a thing. He had heard of men who liked men, but this was the first one he'd met and hopefully the last. "Jawad. As I said before, I'm sorry to disappoint you, but I'm not interested in—" he cleared his throat, "fucking with you or anyone else." Except Kate, he added silently. "I just want to get out of here and back to the dancers' room."

From a happy, expectant smile, Jawad's face fell. "What a disappointment." He spread his hands. "You are such a pretty man."

"Thank you." Maybe the guy wouldn't turn him in after all. Will circled the suite once more, yet he didn't find another door out besides the one he'd originally entered. He would have to figure out how to get past the guard without calling too much attention to himself. "It's been nice knowing you."

"You will not stay and dance for Jawad?"

"Not this time. Maybe next time." Perhaps in another life, but not this one.

Jawad shook his head with a sorrowful expression on his face. "Such a disappointment."

Will pinned the scarf back over his face and opened the door. As he stepped through, he felt a hard slap on his ass. Startled, he turned back.

Jawad shrugged, a guilty smile lifting the corners of his lips. "I cannot resist."

Will scowled at him in warning not to do it again and then he turned his attention to the guard who stood with a rifle in front of his chest. Taking a deep breath, Will hitched a hip out and batted his painted eyelids. In high-pitched, stilted Farsi, he asked, "Could you take me back to my room?"

The guard grunted and motioned for Will to move in front of him.

Schooling his strides to a short, feminine length, he moved down the hallway, forcing a sway to his hips. How did women walk like this? He felt like he would topple over if anyone so much as said boo!

As they passed room after room, he wondered where Kate was and if she'd been successful finding the Eye of the Serpent. He wished he could help her and perhaps he would, after he got rid of the guard.

* * * * *

"Why did you want to leave the dinner so quickly? I was enjoying the dancers." Edie said. "Except the big one." She shivered. "She was so big, she gave me the creeps."

"Probably because *she* wasn't a '*she*'."

"What do you mean?"

Happiness welled up inside. "I'd bet my life that was William Moreland."

"William? Your friend who was with you when you found the Stone of Azhi?"

"The one and only." The man who'd accompanied him on more digs than anyone else. His pal since they were kids in school together. The only man he loved like a brother.

"I would never have thought to look beneath veils to find your friend," Edie said, a skeptical frown denting her brow.

"Me either." A grin slipped across his face as he recalled how hard Will tried to get his attention and the incredibly silly way he shook his hips. When they got out of this mess, he'd have great fodder for future ribbing. If they got out alive. "We have to find him and get back to the Stone of Azhi."

"We still have to find Mitch, too."

"Maybe Will knows where Mitch is."

"Only one way to find out." Edie straightened her shoulders and stood tall.

"Are you with me? Or would you rather stay here where it's relatively safe?"

She planted her fists on her hips. "I'm on this adventure with you, Harrington Taylor the Third. Don't even think about leaving me behind."

"Good." He gathered her in his arms and kissed the tip of her nose. "I like having you around. Besides the convenient sex, you're growing on me."

Edie slapped him on the arm and then took charge of a scorching kiss. When she broke away, her breath was coming in shallow gasps. And so was his.

"Where is the shy and inexperienced Edith Ragsdale I met just a few short days ago?" he asked.

"Gone." The single word was accompanied by a determined look.

"Good. I want more of those kisses. That one alone singed me all the way down to my socks."

With a sexy wink, she responded, "As I've said before, I'm a quick learner."

"That you are." He hugged her and then set her away, her hand still clasped in his. "You want to do the honors?"

"Do you think we will be missed?"

"Maybe a little, but do you care?"

She shrugged. "Not really."

He waved a hand in a sweeping gesture. "Then do your magic."

"It would be my pleasure." She tipped her head to the side. "And what exactly would you like me to wish?"

"To go where Will is."

"I wish for Harry and me to go where Will is." She smiled. "Did I do that right?"

"Perfect." As he leaned over and kissed her lips, the floor wobbled and thunder boomed. "Hold on, we're in for an exciting ride."

She kissed him back and purred in a sexy voice, "It's always an exciting ride with you, Harry."

* * * * *

When Kate landed on her feet in Sheik Sayyid's treasure trove, she rolled behind an ornate display case, ducking low to keep from being detected.

The cavernous room stretched over a football field in length with high ceilings, ornate furniture and display cases artistically positioned throughout. On the walls hung original works of art from revered painters like Picasso, Monet and Van Gogh. The glass display cases contained bejeweled crowns, golden goblets, ancient Ming vases and even Faberge eggs from Russia. One entire section of a wall held a tribute to every sword imaginable from scimitars to Spanish steel from the Renaissance.

Kate gazed around in awe. How did one man have so much and still want more? Money could do that to a person. Loads of money generated from oil wells. While the rich got richer, so many residents of the oil-rich countries lived impoverished lives.

So far, she hadn't seen a guard and her close perusal didn't indicate motion sensors. Perhaps the sheik considered his stash secure with guards posted at the entrances. Or the doors had special locks and she couldn't get out through them. Not that she was worried. As soon as she located the Eye of the Serpent, she'd wish herself out the way she'd come in.

But first, she had to find the jewel that purportedly held the power to free her father and the people of Sand City. Tingles spread across her nerve endings. She was here, in the same room as her father's salvation. The culmination of a year's worry and work to find him. With Will's help and God willing, she'd free her father before the day was over. She dared to let the excitement bubble up inside, before she tamped it down and concentrated on her goal.

Kate stood and moved around the room, not exactly sure what the Eye of the Serpent was supposed to look like. All she had to go on was a black-and-white drawing from an ancient scroll.

When she'd wished to be in the same room as the Eye of the Serpent, she hadn't realized how vast the room would be or how many display cases one man could own. Finding the Eye would take her all day, at this rate.

"I wish I knew exactly which case the Eye was in," she whispered softly.

Kate welcomed the all too familiar floor shaking and thunder booming. Before the echoes diminished, her feet moved without her conscious effort. At first, the movement spooked her. She couldn't stop from moving forward and around objects. Whatever force drove her forward controlled her. Kate wasn't so sure she liked something else controlling her. But if it got her to her destination, so be it. Rather than fight the invisible strings attached to her body, she gave in and allowed herself to be led through the maze of precious gems and art.

In the center of the gallery stood a pedestal of black polished granite. A crystal dome rested on top of the granite platform reflecting the light from the many chandeliers scattered across the ceiling. Within the sparkling glass was a dark topaz jewel surrounded by gold in the shape of an eye. The topaz was different than any Kate had ever seen. Light gold on the outer edges, it grew darker toward the middle until the topaz was a thin black line like the eye of a cat.

The beauty of the jewel outshone every other treasure within the sheik's holding.

Now that she stood within reach of the Eye of the Serpent, Kate hesitated. All the action adventure movies she'd grown up with came back to her. If she removed the Eye of the Serpent from beneath the crystal dome, would she set off an alarm that would bring all the guards in the palace to the gallery? Or would poisoned darts shoot up from the floor and kill her instantly?

Her imagination going wild, she didn't hear the voices until almost too late.

"I trust you did not encounter difficulties in attaining the Eye of the Serpent?" a man's voice said from across the room.

Kate dove beneath a mammoth table and crouched in the shadows.

Sheik Sayyid approached the domed display with Qarim beside him. The two guards she'd seen dragging the thief down the hallways followed close behind.

Head held high, Qarim appeared a little full of himself. "Nothing I could not handle."

"And no one knows you delivered the object to my palace?" the sheik asked.

Qarim bowed his head. "I came in complete secrecy."

Sayyid pressed his fingertips together and nodded. "Ah, that is good."

"Sheik Sayyid, there is the matter of the woman from whom I stole the jewel." Qarim clasped his hands together in front of him. "I fear she will attempt to retrieve the gem from you."

The sheik snorted. "My security system will disallow this occurrence."

"She is a very determined woman," Qarim insisted.

"And my security system is deadly." He nodded toward the dome. "Even should she make it inside my gallery, the domed display is wired to dispense toxic gas if it is lifted without turning the system off. One breath and she will be dead."

Kate's heart leaped in her chest, lodging in her throat. If Sheik Sayyid hadn't come when he did, she'd be dead. And her father would be forever entombed in Sand City. A tear squeezed out the side of her eye and traveled down her cheek. How could she be so careless? Her life meant nothing, but her father deserved to be freed. If she didn't do it, no one would.

Sheik Sayyid and Qarim moved away from the pedestal and back toward the door.

Kate remained immobile until she couldn't hear anything except the pounding of her pulse behind her eardrums. Finally, she emerged from beneath the table to stand in front of the crystal dome. How was she going to take the Eye without dying in the process? No matter what, she had to try. Her father's freedom depended on her succeeding in this venture.

Still, she hesitated, fear piercing her heart. Would she live to free her father? Would she live to make love with Will again? Her nipples and pussy tingled in anticipation of another round of passion from the one-hundred-six-year-old sex god. The thought of not seeing Will again hurt as much as the thought of not seeing her father. She'd never felt this way about a man before Will.

How had he slipped beneath the barriers she'd erected around her heart in such a short amount of time?

Unfortunately, she didn't have time to ponder this conundrum. The longer she waited, the greater the chance of being discovered and of Will being exposed for the man he was. Kate couldn't fail her father and she couldn't allow harm to come to Will.

If inhaling the toxins would kill, she just wouldn't inhale. She breathed in and out several times to steady her nerve. "I wish I were with Will," she said. Then she took a deep breath and held it. Yanking the crystal dome off the pedestal, she threw it across the room where it crashed against the marble floor. Gas rose from tiny holes in the granite previously hidden beneath the rim of the crystal dome.

As the floor rocked beneath her feet, thunder filled the air.

Just before her vision faded, Kate grabbed the Eye of the Serpent.

* * * * *

Will's guard escorted him back into the room where the dancers dressed. As soon as the guard left, Will scoured the suite for another way out. Unfortunately, there wasn't. The only way out was through the guard. Gathering his courage and strength, he reached for the doorknob. Before his hand met the metal, his world tilted and thunder rent the air. Had Kate made a wish? He spun in a circle, willing the black-haired beauty to appear in front of him. Come on, Kate, appear!

Instead of the beautiful Kate, a dark-haired man and that red-haired woman smoked into sight.

"Harry!" Will lunged forward and hugged his friend. "Son of a bitch! Damn, it's good to see you." He blinked back the moisture in his eyes. In a world gone completely insane, Harry's familiar face was like seeing long-lost family. Hell, Harry was all the family Will had now *or* back in 1924.

Harry pounded him on the back and then held him at arm's length. "It's good to see you, too, Will."

"What the hell's been going on?" Will asked. "And give me the short version."

"Fair enough." Harry pounded Will on the back once again, before releasing him, a grin stretching from ear to ear. "It seems, Will, my man, that when a man touches the Stone of Azhi he's trapped in one of those bottles we found in Princess Vashti's tomb."

Will nodded. "That's pretty much what I'd come up with. I had hoped my assumption would be terribly wrong. So, how do we fix it?"

"We have to get all the bottles and the stone back in the tomb of Vashti to break the curse. Do you still have your bottle?"

"No. It's back in the hotel where Kate and I met."

For the first time since Will had hugged Harry, the redhead spoke. "Who's Kate?"

"Kate's the woman who woke me from my bottle."

"Ahh. She and I have a lot in common." The redhead stuck her hand out. "Since Harry has forgotten his manners, let me introduce myself. I'm Edie Ragsdale. I woke Harry from his bottle."

Harry shrugged, "Sorry." He wrapped an arm around Edie's waist and pulled her against him. "She's more than the woman who freed me from the bottle. I know you will think I got hit in the head, but I love this woman." With a smile, he leaned over and kissed her lips.

"You do, don't you?" Edie's eyes misted.

"Nice to meet you." Will cleared his throat. "You two mind? We have bigger problems."

"You're right." Harry sighed and set Edie away. "We still have to find Mitch and the remaining bottles in order to break the curse."

"Whoa, wait a minute." Will held out a hand. "Who is Mitch?"

"He's the guy who helped me and Edie when Danorah Hakala tried to steal the Stone of Azhi."

"Who the hell are Mitch and Danorah? I'm confused." Will pushed his hand through his hair, dislodging the pins holding the veils in place. "All I want to know right now is where's Kate?"

"How should we know?" Harry asked. "Is she in trouble?"

Will paced across the room and back. Should he tell Harry what Kate was up to and risk him turning her in? He glanced at Harry, the man he trusted with his life. Harry wouldn't turn Kate in, especially to the sheik. "At this moment I'd bet she's stealing the Eye of the Serpent from Sheik Sayyid's collection."

"Stealing?" Edie's eyes widened. "Does she realize what he might do to her if he catches her stealing?"

Will's chest tightened. "Yeah. We saw him slit a guy's throat earlier today for stealing food."

Harry pressed his fingers to his temples. "And she's stealing one of his possessions from his art collection?"

Will sighed. "I'm afraid so."

"Your Kate must be out of her mind," Edie said.

Harry grinned. "Either that or she's one very determined woman."

"Obstinate, argumentative and downright pigheaded if you ask me," Will groused. Beautiful, brave and indomitable. "The woman thinks the Eye of the Serpent will help her to find and rescue her father. And I promised to help her."

"You volunteered to help her steal this Eye of the Snake?" Harry asked.

"Serpent," Will corrected. "And yes."

Edie sighed. "She must be pretty special."

"She is." An image of Kate dancing around in the miniscule harem costume flashed across his mind, followed quickly by her eager face encouraging him to join her quest. His mind was consumed with the woman. He had been doomed since the first moment he met her.

Pounding Will on the back, Harry said, "Will, I think you're in love."

"How can that be? I've only known the woman for a day!"

"Intense situations tend to force people closer quickly," Edie said, shooting a knowing smile at Harry.

"I can vouch for that." Harry pulled Edie into his arms and kissed her soundly.

Once again, the floor moved beneath Will's feet and thunder reverberated off the thick walls.

"I think that might be your woman, Will," Harry said.

Will stood still, scanning the room for where Kate would appear. When she faded into view, he stepped forward ready to pull her into a tight embrace.

Before he could, she raised a hand, her gaze darting around the room. Then she ran to the other side of the curtain separating the living quarters from the bathing quarters.

Will followed. As he rounded the heavy drapes, he heard a splash. "What the hell?"

Kate surfaced in the middle of the pool, water streaming from her hair and eyes. When she saw him, she grinned and lifted her hand. A deep golden-brown stone surrounded in gold shone in overhead lights. "I got it!" She hugged herself and dropped back into the pool.

When she came up this time, she walked up the steps leading out. The turquoise sequins on her costume bra sparkled with moisture, reflecting the sparkle in her eyes.

"Why the bath?" Will asked.

"One of Sayyid's security measures was poisonous gas." She reached for one of Will's scarves and dried the Eye.

"Poisonous gas!" Will grabbed her arms and stared down into her face. "Are you all right?"

"I'm fine. I didn't breathe it, and I jumped into the water to rinse off the residue." She smiled at him like a child who'd pulled one over on her teacher.

"Good God, Kate, you could have been killed!" He pulled her into his arms and squeezed her tight. His chest constricted at the thought of Kate lying in some room in the palace, her face pale, her heart stopped. Will hugged her harder.

"Lighten up, Will. I'm all right." She laughed up into his face. "I would have had to breathe it to die. That's why I was holding my breath when I wished myself here."

Will shook his head. "You idiot. You careless, silly idiot. Of all the stupid things to do—" His words were stemmed by Kate's hand over his mouth.

"You did not just call me an idiot, did you?" She moved her hand for his answer.

"I did and that's not all I'll call you." He poked a finger against her chest. "I can't believe you risked poisonous gas to retrieve that stupid Eye."

She bumped her chest against his finger. "And I can't believe you're chewing my ass when I found the damned thing and got out without dying."

"Excuse me…" Harry held up a hand.

Will ignored his friend and continued his tirade. "Of all the pigheaded, obstinate women in the world, my time or yours, I ended up with the queen bee of risk-takers."

"Damn right!" she yelled in a really loud whisper. "And I'd do it all again. I *will* find my father no matter *what* it takes." She poked her finger into his chest. "With or without you, William Moreland."

"Is this making you as hot as it is me?" Will glared, a smile pulling at the corners of his lips.

"Hotter."

"Still, you make me mad, woman." Will fought to maintain his anger, but the more he argued with Kate, the harder he got.

"And you make me even madder." She hooked a wet leg around one of his and rubbed her crotch on him.

"Will!" Harry clamped a hand on his shoulder. "Edie can hear the other women coming back. The guards may come as well."

Knocking the hand off his shoulder, Will leaned into Kate. "I'm not finished here."

"Perhaps you two can continue it outside the palace?" Harry suggested.

Kate dropped her leg and shot him a sly grin. "I think we're finished."

"Oh no we're not." Will knew he hadn't had enough of Kate by a long shot. When they got out of there, he had a bone or two to pick with her. And he looked forward to it. His tone softened. "Look, Kate, you worry me. I don't want you to get hurt."

"Yeah, right. You don't want me to get hurt because you have no idea what will happen to you if I die."

"No. I don't want you to get hurt because, despite your waspish tongue, I like having you around."

Edie raced around the curtain and said in a low voice, "Harry, they're back. We need to go."

As if noticing for the first time that there were others in the bathing room besides them, Kate blinked at Edie and Harry. "Yes, we should go before the entire palace comes down on us. I'm pretty sure the alarms were set off when I stole the Eye."

Will shook his head. "Now she tells us."

"Well, if you hadn't started an argument, I might have gotten around to telling you." When Kate inhaled to spew more words at Will, he leaned forward and clamped his lips to hers, stemming the flow.

When he broke off the kiss, he smiled at the way Kate stood with a dazed expression on her face. "Wish us someplace safe."

"But—"

He pressed another kiss to her lips. "No buts."

"Okay." Kate stared at Edie and Harry. "Who are you?"

"We'll make the introductions later."

"But I'm not sure I can wish them out of here with us."

Edie rested a hand on Kate's arm. "You don't have to. Just tell us where you're going and I'll take care of the rest."

"Can you—?"

"Yes." Voices could be heard in the other room and Edie glanced toward the edge of the curtain before saying. "We better hurry."

"But what about Will's bottle?" Harry asked. "Shouldn't we get it and put it in a safe place before we join them?"

Will frowned. "Not that I'm going soft or anything, but now that I have you back in my life, I don't want to lose you again, Harry."

Harry smiled. "Same, buddy. But if we are going to have any chance of freeing ourselves from this wish nonsense, we have to return all the bottles and the stone to the tomb of Vashti."

Dread screamed inside Will, but on the outside he nodded. "Okay, but don't take too long. We might need help getting Kate's father out of Sand City."

"Sand City it is. We'll be right behind you." Harry held out a hand to Will. "Take care out there."

With a quick jerk, Will pulled Harry into his arms and hugged him. "Same for you."

"Okay, then." Kate glanced up at Will and squinted her eyes like she was about to do something Will wasn't going to like. "I have no idea what to expect on the other side of the wish I'm about to make."

"Just don't get us into more trouble, Kate." Will might as well have been spitting in the wind. Kate would do anything to get her father back. "You really love your father, don't you?"

"He's the only family I have left," she said quietly.

Will nodded, his lips firming into a straight line. "Then let's go get him."

With a broad grin and a rush of words she made her wish. "I wish Will and I were at the gate to Sand City."

Edie grabbed Harry's hand. "I wish Harry and I were where Will's bottle is."

The room tipped and the floors trembled beneath Will's feet. As his vision blurred, Will asked, "Is Sand City anywhere near Hell?"

Chapter Eight

ജ

Blistering heat bore down on Will and Kate as they stood in the direct sun. Sand stretched for as far as Kate could see—miles and miles of sand—gritty, biting sand when wind gusts sent it blasting through the air.

"Great, Kate, the joke's on us, Sand City is another name for Hell." Will yanked one of the veils off his belt and held it over his and Kate's head. "So? Where's your city?"

"I don't know. The legend says it is invisible to those who can't see past the sand."

Will turned in a complete circle. "Then we're in trouble. All I can see is sand. Can you see anything?"

As she stared around the barren terrain, tears welled in Kate's eyes. "This has to be it. I wished us to be at the gate to Sand City. For all I know, my father could be somewhere nearby."

Will released one end of his scarf and circled her waist with his arm, setting all joking aside. "Maybe there's a magic word you have to use."

"Like open sesame or something?"

"Yeah." He kissed the top of her head. "Try it."

The strength of Will's arm around her gave Kate hope and she looked out across the desert. "Open sesame."

Nothing happened. No city appeared in the sand. Nothing.

"Any other ideas?" she asked, the little bit of hope shriveling in the intense heat.

"How about the Eye of the Serpent?" Will said. "Didn't you say it was the key to Sand City?"

"That's right!" She lifted the golden jewel to the light. Sun shone through the multifaceted jewel, shedding a cascade of light across the sandy desert floor. Still, nothing. No city, not so much as a cornerstone, window, door or broken bottle.

Kate's eyes welled with tears and her arm dropped. "What a waste of time. We've come all this way and fought so hard to retrieve this darn trinket, for what? My father is still missing and I'm out of options."

"Don't give up yet. We'll think of something."

"It's hot, I'm tired and thirsty and this damn bra is giving me a rash. It's no use." She tossed the Eye of the Serpent into the sand. "I wish I'd never come." As she leaned against Will, her sobs almost drowned out the sound of booming thunder. The sand at their feet shifted.

"Oh no, Kate." Will clutched her arms, his eyes wide with panic. "Undo it. Undo it now!"

She glanced up into his face, her gaze confused. "Undo wh—oh. Did I make a w—"

Before her eyes, Will faded into blackness.

* * * * *

Kate stood in the bathing area of the dancers' sleeping quarters in the exact spot she'd been before she'd wished herself and Will to Sand City. In front of her stood at least half the palace guards, Sheik Sayyid and Qarim. Every one of the men stared at her in wonder.

With her stomach burbling, Kate summed up her odds of escaping. At the moment, they looked pretty anemic. She gave a shaky laugh. "Guess you've never seen a woman appear out of thin air, have you?"

Qarim pointed at her. "That is the woman—Kate Ralston—she is the one who will have taken the Eye of the Serpent."

"Is this true?" Sheik Sayyid demanded.

"Can I plead the fifth?" she asked.

The sheik didn't blink.

"No. I didn't think so." Could she have chosen a worse time to feel sorry for herself and make a stupid wish? She fought the gut-wrenching fear creeping into her belly. After a deep breath she opened her mouth to make another wish to get herself out of the mess.

"I wish—" Kate started.

Before she finished her wish, Qarim yelled, "Don't let her speak!"

Sheik Sayyid shouted in Farsi. The guard nearest to her grabbed her and clamped a hand over her mouth.

Now she was in deep quicksand and sinking deeper. Here she was back in Sadistic Sayyid's palace facing the opportunity to have her throat slit. Will was stranded in the desert, probably cursing her. Will's other two friends were probably fat, dumb and happily retrieving that stupid blue-green bottle that started this whole shindig. So who was going to get her out of the dilemma?

"Why not let her speak?" The sheik turned to Qarim.

"Did you see how she appeared out of nowhere?" Qarim asked.

"Yes."

"I think it has to do with wishing." The trader walked a half circle around her, studying her as if she were a flea under a microscope.

If she could, she'd spit in the twerp's eye.

Finally, Qarim turned to the sheik. "Let her talk and I fear you will never see the Eye of the Serpent."

Sheik Sayyid stepped close to her and glared into her face. "Did you steal the Eye of the Serpent?" he demanded.

What did he expect her to say? *I did it! I'm the thief. Here, slit my throat.* With a hand over her mouth, she couldn't say anything so, like the smart girl her father raised, she shook her head and gave the sheik as innocent a look as she could muster.

The sheik frowned. "If you did not steal the Eye, who did?"

"She has to be the one who stole the Eye," Qarim said in a soft, but firm voice.

The sheik leaned into her, his breath smelling of curry. "Where is it? Where is the Eye of the Serpent?"

Kate shrugged and hoped by some miracle Will would find his way back to rescue her from this pickle barrel she'd sunk herself into. Like that was about to happen. He didn't have the ability to wish himself anywhere. She had all the power and it was trapped behind a smelly, meaty hand at the moment.

When Kate couldn't and wouldn't answer, the sheik's face grew redder and he glared down at her. Then he looked at the guards holding her and said in an icy voice, "Kill her."

The guard next to Meaty Paw withdrew a wicked knife from his belt, stepped toward Kate and pressed the blade against her throat. The cold steel cut a path of fear to her heart. Kate braced herself for the pain and the gallons of blood she'd lose. Why, oh why, had she made that stupid wish?

Qarim's eyes narrowed and he placed a hand on the sheik's arm. "No, wait." He stepped forward. "Sheik Sayyid, this woman may know of the archeologists who spoke of the tomb of Vashti. She may also know the whereabouts of the Stone of Azhi."

Sheik Sayyid held up a hand and the guard stopped. "Is this true?"

Should she own up to knowing about the Stone of Azhi and possibly be spared a cold, blade collar? Or should she keep her knowledge to herself, a martyr to Will and his friends? What could it hurt to admit she knew something? What did she really know, anyway? All these thoughts coursed through her brain in the blink of her eye.

Kate nodded.

"What do you know of the Stone of Azhi? And where are the archeologists?" The sheik waved at the guard and the man released his hold on her mouth.

"I don't know much about it, but I wish—"

"Don't let her wish for anything!" Qarim slapped his hand over Kate's mouth.

Angry about being foiled at her second attempt to make a wish, Kate sank her teeth into the man's hand.

"Ouch!" Qarim jerked his hand away.

"I wish I were—" Ol' Meaty Paw clamped his viselike grip over her lips effectively silencing her once again.

Enough was enough. Kate jammed her elbow back into the man's gut, with enough force to bring a normal man to his knees.

The big guy barely grunted.

She tried dropping into a crouch and flinging him over her shoulder.

Ha! The giant didn't budge.

So much for escape.

Qarim stood out of Kate's range, holding his bleeding hand out in front of him, his eyes blazing. "Legend tells of the power of the Stone of Azhi. I think she has the stone's power to wish for anything she wants. You would be wise to gag her and keep her from wishing you to burn in Hell."

You bet my sweet ass. And I can do that. Ask Will what it's like. Kate smiled behind the hand over her mouth. When she got her mouth back to herself, *Look out, Qarim, you're thieving days are over*!

Qarim stared at Kate. "The question is how do we get her to tell us where the Stone of Azhi is if we can't let her mouth go?" He paced a few steps away from her and back toward the sheik keeping his distance from her hands, feet and teeth. "Jawad said the tall dancer he took back to his room was a man."

"A man?" Sheik Sayyid's face flushed red again. "Why is there a man amongst my dancers? Bring him to me!"

Guards moved to obey, but Qarim held up a hand. "I wouldn't bother. Based on the power of the wishes, I'd lay odds he isn't here and neither are the archeologists. And I'll bet this woman knows where they are. Am I right?"

Kate shrugged.

Qarim nodded, a smile slithering across his face. "If we cannot get her to tell us where the stone is, we can hold her captive until the others come back for her. Then they will lead us to the Stone of Azhi or we kill their pretty friend."

The sheik raised a finger. "And the Eye of the Serpent. I want both. The task is simple. Your life for my treasures."

Behind the guard's big hand, Kate gulped. Somehow she had to get her voice back. Even if Sheik Sayyid retrieved both the Stone of Azhi and the Eye of the Serpent, he wouldn't be satisfied until those who chose to steal from him were dead. And the way he sounded, he was lumping Will, Harry and the red-haired woman into the same group with Kate. What had she gotten them all into and how could she get them out of it without her ability to wish?

* * * * *

When Kate disappeared, Will dropped to his knees in the sand and turned his face to the sun-drenched sky. "Damn you, Kate!" She'd left him in the hellhole of a desert to rot. No water, no shade, no damned Sand City.

The golden-brown topaz blinked at him from where Kate had dropped it. With the sun glinting off its surface, the shiny topaz eye mocked him.

She'd worked over a year to find the Eye of the Serpent, so certain it would help her free her father from the legendary Sand City. Will could understand Kate's disappointment. He knew how hard it was to lose your father. He'd lost his father when he was only sixteen.

That's when he'd hooked up with Harry and the rest was history. Practically ancient history. If Will thought his father might still be alive, he'd try everything in his power to bring him back. Like Kate.

He lifted the Eye of the Serpent and turned it over. On the back of the gold casing was an inscription. Will held it up to the sun to read it, but he couldn't make out the words. They were in a language he did not understand. Carved near the top was a two-headed dragon.

While Will held the Eye of the Serpent, the sun descended in the western sky. No, he couldn't make out the words, but the sun's rays eventually reached an angle where they burst through the middle of the gem spreading beams of light in every direction of the prism. At this slant, the shattered light leveled perpendicular to the ground shooting straight out, not downward.

Will's gaze followed the rays, his fascination over the refracted light taking his mind off how hot and thirsty he was. He could do with a palace to duck into about now. One perched in an oasis with a pool sparkling in the afternoon sun. The sand shimmered as a heat wave rose off the hot surface and wobbled in the refracted light generated by the Eye.

If Will weren't careful, he'd start seeing mirages of his current fantasy. That palace he'd been dreaming of a moment ago wavered across his vision, standing tall and white in the middle of an oasis.

Blinking his eyes, Will tried to refocus on the true desert terrain, not this heat-induced image that was nothing more than a figment of his inflamed imagination. But the more he blinked, the more defined the picture became. With the back of his hand, Will rubbed his eyes. "Kate, I could use a second opinion about now. I think I'm losing my mind."

When he glanced out again, the image was still there. If he reached out, would he feel the palace?

No. The hot, dry air and the fading sun had cooked his brain, even more so than his trip to Hell.

As he lowered the Eye of the Serpent, it was as if the light had been turned off. All that stood before him was the empty desert.

See? Just a mirage like the smoke and mirrors of a magician's show. The smoke being the heat from the desert floor, the mirrors the refracted light from the Eye of the Serpent. Will lifted the gem to catch the sun again and the image of the palace appeared. Only this time, a man stood in front of the gated entrance, waving like he was trying to get his attention. Soon there were ten, then twenty, then thirty people waving in front of the palace.

Familiar with the desert from previous archeological expeditions, Will had heard of mirages of desert oases, but never in his life had he heard of mirages including a palace fully equipped with people. He lurched to his feet, losing the optimum angle for the sun to pierce the Eye. The mirage was gone, but Will couldn't shake the feeling the palace wasn't.

His mind must be playing tricks on him—the sun's heat murdering his ability to produce coherent thought. Maybe he could walk toward where the palace was. Not because he believed it was there, but he had this urgent sense that if he didn't he'd always wonder.

Clad in a harem dancer's scarves and satin slippers, Will stepped carefully across the sandy desert floor in the direction he'd seen the mirage, just like a crazed nomad in search of water. He could even smell the water, like a fresh spring rain. Another step and he could swear he felt the gentle spray of a fountain against his skin.

No. Will dug his feet into the sand. He couldn't torture himself like this. Kate would come back for him and if not, Harry and Edie would. If all else failed, he'd find his way out of this desert and back to America. Morelands didn't give up and they didn't go insane over a little desert heat!

But what would it hurt to go a few more steps toward the scent of spring showers? Will stepped forward and stubbed his toe through the thin fabric of the dancer's slipper.

"Ouch!" What the heck? How could he stub his toe in the sand? A glance downward revealed the curve of a solid white column. As his gaze traveled upward, the column towered three stories over the desert floor. It looked more real than any mirage he'd ever imagined and by the throbbing in his big toe, it felt like granite. Stepping to the side he saw the palace in his mirage and dozens of people rushing toward him.

"Okay, now I know I'm losing my mind." Question was, did he close his eyes and assume it was all a dream? Or were these people real, perhaps some of Sheik Sayyid's people looking for the Eye of the Serpent he still carried in his right hand?

With the assumption cities don't just appear in the middle of the desert, Will stood his ground and pretended to himself these people didn't exist. But when the first man reached him and hugged him to his chest, Will could no longer go with his original assumption. This guy was real!

The man was tall, black-haired with little streaks of gray at his temples and piercing blue eyes like Kate's.

"Are you Kate Ralston's father?" Will asked.

"Why yes! I'm Anthony Ralston. Tony to my friends." He grabbed Will's arms. "Do you know Kate? Is she all right? Where is she?" He glanced over Will's shoulder as if expecting to see Kate behind him.

"That's a good question." Will's lips pressed into a tight line. "I'd like to know the answer myself." The longer she'd been gone, the more he believed she might be in trouble. He had to find a way to get to her and help her.

Kate's father ran his gaze up and down Will's length. "I don't get it. You sound like a man, but you're dressed like a woman. Which one is it? Or are you in drag?"

"Drag? What do you mean?" Will shook his head. "Never mind. I am a man, dressed as a woman to hide from a sheik. It's a long story."

"I see." Tony didn't look like he saw anything, a small frown denting his forehead. "So how did you get in here?"

"I stubbed my toe on the column over there." He glanced down at the jewel in his hand. "But I could see you and the rest of these people when I held this jewel up to the light."

Tony grabbed his hand, his grip practically cutting off Will's circulation. "The Eye of the Serpent! Oh, thank God." Without releasing Will's hand, Tony reached out with his empty hand. "May I?"

"Sure." Will handed over the Eye of the Serpent. "Is it true this is the key that will free Sand City?"

"Yes." Tony let go of Will's hand and held the Eye of the Serpent out in front of him like he was afraid he would drop it or maybe he was seeing things. "Once we return the Eye to the statue of the Serpent, Sand City will be free. Generations of people have waited a long time to have the Eye of the Serpent returned. Since the time of Azhi, the Devil King, the people of Sand City have been trapped in the desert."

When Anthony's words sank in, a tingle slithered across Will's nerve endings. "Did you say Azhi?"

"Yes, he was the evil ancient ruler who stole the Eye of the Serpent and condemned Sand City to disappear into the desert when the prince of Sand City broke the heart of Azhi's only daughter."

"His daughter wouldn't happen to be Vashti?"

Tony glanced up, his eyes wide. "Why yes."

"Unfortunately, I've heard of the man and just the mention of his name explains a lot. I think Azhi must have been a very evil king or he loved his daughter very much."

"I think he was both." Tony's smile widened. "Shall we return the Eye to its rightful place and free these good people?"

"By all means." Will thought of all the changes that had occurred in the eighty years he'd been trapped in the bottle. The people of Sand City had been trapped for hundreds of years. "Are they ready for the shock?"

* * * * *

Collecting the bottle had taken a little longer than Harry had expected. When Edie wished them to the location of Will's bottle, they'd ended up in a hotel supply closet with a small vent over the door providing very little light. While searching for the bottle in the tight confines Harry bumped into Edie so much he couldn't help getting aroused. And, well, a nudge led to a stroke and before Harry could think another thought about Will and Kate, he and Edie were tearing their clothes off, impatient to feel skin against skin.

Harry pulled her blouse up and over her head, laying it on a shelf beside her. Then he leaned in and nipped at her nipple through the lacy fabric of her bra.

Edie reached up behind her and unfastened the garment, peeling the straps down over her shoulders. "Is that better?"

"Ummm. Much." His hands slid up her rib cage, his thumbs circling her rosy-tipped breasts until they formed rigid peaks. Then he leaned down and sucked one into his mouth while his hand massaged the other.

Edie moaned, her fingers digging into his hair, holding him closer to her. "You make me ache."

"Honey, you don't know the half of it." His mouth trailed downward, his tongue flicking a path over each rib and lower to her bellybutton.

He couldn't get enough of her. Edie's skin was as smooth as silk and she tasted of the jasmine-scented soap from the sheik's palace. The image of her propped on the side of the pool, her legs open to him, had his cock as hard as granite.

"You're wearing too many clothes," she said and slipped each button open on his shirt with more haste than care. One popped off and clanked against the metal shelving. With a determined yank, she had his shirt out of his waistband and went to work on the hard metal button of his jeans, struggling to release it.

"Allow me." With a flick of his strong fingers, he pushed the button loose and lowered his zipper, afraid if Edie attempted it, she'd damage his penis in the process.

Her hand slipped inside the back of his jeans and down over his buttocks, pulling him against her.

Harry struggled to breathe, afraid he'd come before he pleasured her. And he liked the sounds she made when he brought her to the edge. Where had Edie the museum mouse gone? In her place was Edie the warrior, out to conquer his heart and make love like a wild woman.

Smoothing his hands over her hips, he eased her trousers down her legs, dropping to his knees to lift each foot out of the constraining material. Then he slid her panties down and removed them, setting them to the side where they could be easily found.

His heart raced as he stared up at her in the dim light from the single bulb overhead. "Edie, you're the most beautiful woman I've ever seen."

Her blush rose up her neck and into her cheeks, making her skin glow. "Are you going to stand there and stare or get naked and fuck me?"

Harry jumped to his feet, shucked his jeans and stood naked in front of her. "Is that better?"

"Almost," she said and stepped closer, her hand skimming across his chest, lacing through the curly hairs. She pinched the tips of his hard brown nipples and dropped her hands to his cock, cupping his balls in one palm. "I love how hard you get. It makes me feel sexy."

"You're an incredibly sexy woman, Edie. Do you want me to show you how sexy I think you are?"

"Please," she whispered against his ear.

Tracing the back of his hands along her jawline, he cupped her neck and turned her face up to his. When he claimed her lips, he stepped closer, pressing his rock-hard cock against her belly, loving the feel of her soft skin rubbing against him.

His tongue delved between her lips and wrapped around hers, pushing in and out of her mouth as his hips rocked against hers in the same motion.

She reached around him and clutched his buttocks, kneading the flesh with petite fingers that only stirred his lust to greater depths. He couldn't wait to push inside her cunt and feel the tight walls surrounding his engorged cock. But he wanted her to come first.

With his hands trailing down over her collarbone, he smoothed across her luscious breasts. He paused to tweak the nipples before lowering to cup her in his palms. As he bent to take a tit in his mouth, she reached between them and circled his cock with both hands.

He almost lost it there. Harry dragged in a deep, steadying breath before he continued his assault on her body. While his hands skimmed down her sides, he dropped to his knees and pressed a kiss to the mound of reddish-blonde hair covering her mons. "I want to fuck you, Edie."

"Quit talking and do it!" she gasped, spreading her legs wider.

"Not yet. I want you to want me as much as I want you."

She laughed out loud. "Sounds like a lot of double talk, if you ask me." Her words came out in a rush, as if she were running a marathon and couldn't get enough air. "I'm already wet and ready. Please, fuck me," she cried.

"Not yet," he repeated. "Patience, sweetheart. I promise you will have no regrets."

He rubbed his cock against her mound, parting the folds with the hard ridge until his penis connected with her clit.

She reached behind her, her fingers gripping the shelf on either side of her hips. "Oh my…oh my…that feels so good."

Smiling, he lowered his face to brush between her breasts, the stubble on his chin scraping against her soft skin.

Her hands rose to cup his ears, pressing his face closer before she pushed him downward.

A chuckle escaped him. He loved how she took control when he didn't move fast enough for her liking. And he loved torturing her until she was in a frothing frenzy. But he allowed her to direct his descent lower until his tongue traced a path through the soft hairs over her pussy. Gently nudging her folds aside with his tongue, he tasted her clit, flicking it until she gasped her hands alternating between pulling his head closer and pushing him away. "Do you want more?" he asked, blowing a stream of cool air against her damp cunt.

"Oh yes!" she said, reaching down between them to part her nether lips to give him better access to her.

As he tongued her, swirling around the swollen nub, he ran his thumbs up the insides of her thighs until they converged at the opening to her vagina. He pushed both thumbs into her wet cunt, splaying the opening wider. Then he dropped his head lower and slid his tongue inside her as deep as he could go.

Her thighs clamped around his ears and he tongued harder, mimicking the in-and-out motion of fucking her. Her musky taste incited a riot in his loins and he fought to maintain control.

Edie cried out and dug her nails into his back, her pussy rising up to meet his tongue's thrusts.

He replaced his tongue with three fingers and moved back to tease her clit until she wrapped her legs around his shoulders and screamed. Her body pulsed with her release.

Before Edie's fires abated, Harry shoved her legs from his shoulders and stood, sliding his throbbing cock into her cunt, filling her channel until his balls bumped into her ass. Fully sheathed, he paused, sucking in a deep breath. Then he pulled out until only the tip of his penis touched her creamy opening.

Her knees lifted and she wrapped her heels around his waist, digging them into his lower back, pulling him into her. "Fuck me, Harry."

"As you wish." He pumped in and out of her until he shot over the edge, spilling his seed into her. They collapsed against the shelving unit, breathing hard, but satiated.

"I love you, Edie," he said as he gathered her into his arms without sliding his cock out of her.

Her legs tightened around his waist as her arms circled his neck. "I love you too, Harry."

A few moments later, Edie's feet lowered to the ground and they returned to reality.

Harry sighed as he zipped his jeans. "You amaze me."

Edie stopped in the process of fastening her bra around her waist and reached out to cup Harry's cheek. With a saucy grin she said, "You make me amaze myself." She pressed a kiss to his lips and pressed her bare breasts to his equally naked chest.

His waning cock responded to the stimulus, hardening beneath denim and the metal zipper. "We really should get back to help Will and Kate. They might be in danger again."

She traced a finger down the center of his chest to the thin line of hair disappearing beneath his waistband. "They're tough. They can handle a few more minutes without us." With a twist of her fingers, the thick metal button released.

How could he resist this redheaded vixen? "You're right. Kate can wish them out of any difficulties."

"But you can't wish yourself out of the trouble you're about to be in," she said.

"You don't see me trying, do you?"

Her hand slid into his jeans and down to cup his balls.

Harry drew in a deep breath and pressed himself against her, pushing her back against the shelf behind her. His hands slipped up her sides to cup her breasts, kneading the nipples into tight little nubs.

She pulled her hand from his pants and planted both fists on her hips. "Oh no you don't. It's my turn to touch you." Her gaze narrowed. "I wish your hands were tied to the shelf behind you."

The requisite floor shaking and thunder rumbling sent a shot of adrenaline through Harry's system. If he could, he'd run from this latest wish. The next thing he knew, his wrists were bound to the metal shelving behind him. "I don't know about this, Edie," he said, tugging at the ropes. "Sometimes your wishes backfire."

"Relax." She pressed her breasts against him again. "Now where was I?" She dropped to her knees and spread his fly wide. "Ah, yes. I was here." In one long, drawn-out movement, she pushed his jeans and boxers down around his ankles.

"How am I supposed to get anything out of this with my hands tied above my head?" His cock stood at attention, belying Harry's words. All he had to do was see Edie naked and he got hard.

"Don't you remember?" She ran a finger around the head of his penis. "The time you tied me to my bed?"

Teeth grinding together, Harry tried to slow the blood flowing south to his groin. "I was hoping you'd have forgotten that little incident."

"How could I?" She touched her tongue to his cock and fire lit him from within.

"Edie, let me go. If someone walks in, how would this look?" Harry didn't argue with much starch behind his words. The wonderful things she was doing to him had his head swimming and his penis as hard as iron. "We're in a foreign country where women are submissive."

"Even more of a reason to do this. I'm kinda liking that thrill of danger." She knelt before him, the weak light striping her pale skin.

Harry longed to take her in his arms and ram his cock deep inside her until she begged him to stop. But he was completely at her mercy. And he was enjoying it more than he cared to admit.

When Edie wrapped her lips around him, he surged forward, filling her mouth until the tip of his penis bumped against the back of her throat.

"Mmm." She backed off him until cool air met his moist, hot penis. Then with her tongue she licked him from the base of his cock to the tiny hole at the top, sucking the tip into her mouth, teasing a drop of come from him.

Harry wanted to reach out and cup her tits in his hands, to wrap her thighs around his waist and ram inside her and fuck her until he'd spent himself. But he was tied to a shelf, immobile except for his legs and hips.

Edie rose to stand in front of him, far enough away she didn't touch him. "Did you like that?'"

He looked down at his engorged cock. "You know the answer to that."

Her hand wrapped around him, her fingers tangling in the hair around his balls. "What would you like next?"

"I want to fuck you until you scream," he said.

Her breasts rose and fell as she gasped. "I love it when you talk dirty to me. But I get to fuck you this time."

"Then do it before I explode."

Edie climbed up him, wrapping her arms around his neck and her legs around his waist. Then she lowered her cunt over him until the moist lips of her vagina hovered just about the tip of his cock. "How do you want it, slow and easy, or hot and fast?" she whispered into his ear, nipping at the earlobe.

Harry bucked beneath her, his cock straining to enter that warm, wet channel. "Hot and fast. Make it hot and fast!"

Edie sank down over him. Then bracing her arms on his shoulders and leveraging the shelves behind him, she moved up and down hot and fast.

"Come with me, Edie," he said as he shot over the edge. He strained against the ropes his entire body so tense every muscle screamed. Had he been anywhere else but a storage room in a hotel, Harry might have screamed as well.

Her arms choking off his air, Edie stopped and held on, her body jerking to the rhythm of her orgasm.

Before either could catch their breath, the door burst open and light flooded into the tiny room, exposing the guilty, naked couple to the harsh light.

A woman stood silhouetted against the hall lights, her hands on her hips and her feet spread slightly apart. "Ha! I have you now."

The voice was too familiar and when she flipped the light switch on, Harry's suspicions were confirmed.

Danorah Hakala had caught up with them.

"What the hell?" Edie climbed down from Harry and grabbed for her clothing.

"Don't worry about your clothes, Edie. Get us the hell out of here," Harry shouted.

"Grab them!" Danorah screamed. "And don't let the woman talk."

With her clothes clutched to her chest, Edie's gaze darted from Harry to Danorah. "I wish Harry and I—"

A man reached into the storage room and yanked her out by the hair.

"Yeeoow!" Edie kicked and flailed against the much larger man, hauling her out by the hair.

Harry struggled against his bonds. "Edie!" His heart leaped into his throat as she was dragged farther away from him.

Before Edie could get another word out, the man slapped a hand over her mouth and clamped her arms to her sides. Her struggles were futile against the man's bulk and brawn.

"Let her go. I'll give you what you want."

Danorah laughed a hard, derisive laugh. "I doubt that you can give me what I want."

"If you hurt one hair on her head, I'll kill you."

Danorah snarled. "You can do nothing, by the looks of it." She crossed her arms over her chest, her gaze traveling the length of Harry's body. "Not bad." Then she turned to Edie and cupped one of her breasts. "But my preferences go toward softer flesh." She squeezed Edie's tit until Edie's eyes watered. "That's right. I have plans for you, my dear."

"Leave her alone." Harry kicked out with his feet, but was brought up short by the ties around his wrists. "Damn!"

"Having difficulties?" Danorah laughed again.

The sound grated against Harry's eardrums and he glared at her. "What do you want?"

"Oh, I think you know what I want." Danorah's hand trailed down Edie's body to slide beneath her legs.

"The Stone of Azhi isn't there," Harry said between tight lips.

"Then I suggest you go get it." She leaned over Edie and licked her breast and then she bit down hard.

Edie bucked beneath the heavy hands of Danorah's henchman, her feet flailing out toward Danorah.

But the bleached-blonde stepped back in time to avoid being hit, a smile curving her lips. "You better hurry back before I rape her. And if you take too long, not only will I rape her, I'll kill her."

"How am I supposed to go if I'm still tied up?"

She snorted. "That would be your problem, not mine."

Chapter Nine

Kate sat bound to a chair, gagged with one of the scarves she'd been wearing. How the hell would she get out of this mess without a major miracle? Qarim had stationed four guards to watch over her at all times.

Even if Edie could wish Harry and Will into the same room, they couldn't stand up to the strength of these goons. They were huge.

But she couldn't give up. Not now. What if Harry and Edie didn't make it back to Will? He'd be stuck in the desert with no water or transportation. He'd die.

Tears welled in Kate's eyes. She didn't want Will to die. He was growing on her. She liked the way he argued with her over everything. It completely turned her on. The thought of him fucking her like a whore surfaced and sent her blood flowing southward throughout her body, causing her cunt to weep.

If she got out of this alive, she wanted to make love to Will again. Only this time, she'd let him do it the way he wanted.

Which brought up a good point. Did he even want to make love to her? The last couple times she'd wished him to make love to her. Would he do it on his own?

Would she ever find out?

She rocked the chair, twisting her hands, trying to pull free of her silk bindings. But she only managed to tighten them. What was the use? Her head dropped forward and she blinked her eyes, the strain of the day and all that had happened draining her energy. One yawn beneath the gag led to another. Each time her mouth got drier and drier. Finally, she fell into a fitful sleep where her father and Will had met and were discussing all her faults. As if!

How long she slept, she didn't know, but a tinkling noise broke through the barrier of sleep and Kate looked up.

Haley, Moira and a dozen of the dancing girls had entered the room, smiling, giggling and fully costumed in their belly-dancer outfits.

When the guards moved toward them to usher them back out, the ladies started to dance, their golden belts riding extra low on hips that rocked back and forth. The guards stopped in their tracks, their gazes fully focused on those gyrating hips and the sparkling, sequined bras.

The women gave the guards the same show they'd given the sheik, only they got a little more explicit in order to keep the guards' attention. Three or more women surrounded each guard, peeling scarves off one by one and wrapping them around the guards' heads in a blatantly seductive dance.

One of the guards stood with his arms crossed over his chest, his eyes staring forward, refusing to reach out for one of the lovelies. The three other guards were completely entranced by Haley and her girls. They reached out to tug on the colorful scarves in hopes of bringing one of the women within squeezing range.

Kate watched in awe, as the women weaved a spell of seduction around the men. Even though Kate loved what men had to offer, she couldn't help being a little turned on by the movements of the beautiful women.

No matter how much they turned and twisted, shaking their breasts in suggestive ways, the one stoic guard refused to take his gaze off Kate.

Haley and Moira converged on him with their own style of temptation when Haley unclasped Moira's bra and dropped it to the floor.

Moira gasped, feigning surprise and covered her bare breasts.

The guard glanced at her perky tits. Once hooked he couldn't look away. Haley and Moira put on a show he'd not soon forget. Haley slipped up behind Moira and encircled her waist, running her hands up to fondle the other woman's breasts.

Moira shrieked and playfully slapped the hands away. Then Haley slid her hands over Moira's flat stomach and down into the sequined bottoms.

Instead of fighting, Moira leaned back against Haley and moaned.

The guard's eyes widened and his gaze zeroed in on the hand Haley had tucked into Moira's panties. When Moira moaned again, the guard's face reddened and he tugged at the collar of his robes.

In the meantime, one of the ladies slipped away from the guards and circled behind Kate, running her hands over Kate's shoulders and down into her bra. What was she doing? Whatever it was, felt pretty damn good. Kate's breasts tightened and her pussy creamed. If only it were Will's rough hands instead.

One of the guards glanced her way, his eyes narrowed. From across the room, Moira moaned loud enough to cut through the jingling bangles draping the women's wrists and hips. Moira had turned in Haley's arms and removed Haley's top. She was in the process of sucking one of the brunette's nipples into her mouth while Haley pushed her hands down her own pants to rub against her clit. All male eyes riveted on the two women making love in the middle of the room.

The woman behind Kate quickly untied the scarf gagging Kate's mouth.

Her heart in her throat and a little disappointed she couldn't stick around for the rest of the show, Kate whispered, "I wish I were with Will." When the floor shook and thunder rumbled, Kate glanced once more at the two half-naked women. She fervently hoped they didn't catch a lot of flack for freeing her. And Kate hoped Will was in the mood for a little fucking, because she sure was. And if she had to wish him into the mood, after what she had been through, she considered it justified.

* * * * *

Will stayed in Sand City not a second longer than was necessary to replace the Eye in the Serpent statue. From what Anthony had told him, it would take two days of hard riding to get back to Riyadh. Two long days away from Kate and he had no idea what kind of trouble she'd landed in.

Until the Eye made it back to its proper place, Will couldn't leave Sand City, and neither could anyone else. Without giving the people a chance to perform a ceremony or mark the day in history, Will climbed up on the two-story Serpent, jammed the jewel in the Serpent's eye socket and climbed back down.

When he reached the ground, Anthony Ralston hugged him. "Thank you for saving our lives and freeing us from exile."

"Thank me after we free your daughter." Will wondered if Anthony would be thanking him once he learned he'd fucked his daughter like a whore. He'd keep that little bit of information to himself.

"What can we do to help?" Anthony asked.

"If I could get some transportation out of here, that would help."

An hour later, Will left the palace in traditional Arab garb of white robes and the *kaffiyeh* headdress, thankful to be shielded from the harsh desert sun and ecstatic to be out of the harem girl outfit. Perched on top of an albino camel that smelled like…well…a camel, he galloped through the palace gates. Gallop might have been using the term loosely. Lumbering along having your insides jolted beyond recognition wasn't something Will considered galloping. From his forays into Iraq, Will had gained a respect for camels, having had some spit in his eye on more occasions than he cared to count. He preferred horses when automobiles weren't available. From a community that had spent nearly a thousand years confined to an invisible oasis in the desert, Will counted his blessings that he could coax them to lend their only camel to his mission.

Balancing the compass Anthony Ralston had given him, Will hoped he was headed in the right direction to find the sheik's palace on the outskirts of Riyadh. Kate's father had argued long and hard to come with him, but Will reasoned that the camel would move faster with only one passenger. And once he found Kate, he knew he stood a better chance of fighting off her captors than the older man. His gut clenched when he thought of what Sheik Sayyid might be doing to Kate.

He hadn't gone more than a mile when something heavy grabbed around his neck with a stranglehold. Struggling to breathe, Will hauled back on the reins, bringing the camel to a skidding halt in the sand.

Whatever had him by the throat clung to him and he fought to detach the viselike grip. When he loosened the hold, his attacker slid off the back of the camel.

Black hair and belly-dancer sequins flashed by as his attacker landed with a thud on the desert floor. "Kate!"

"Thanks!" Kate scrambled from beneath the shifting camel feet and stood, dusting herself off. Then she propped her hands on her hips and stared up at Will. "What kind of hero are you, anyway? Did you have to go and dump me off the back of that giant goat?"

He leaped from the camel's back and landed on the ground beside her, gathering her stiff body into his arms.

"Kate!" he said again. He couldn't believe it was her out here in the middle of nowhere. "I had no idea what happened to you."

"Is that any reason to dump me onto the desert floor?" She rubbed her backside and then threw her arms around his neck.

After several minutes of hugging and kissing, Will set her away from him and frowned down into her face. "Why the hell did you leave me stranded in the desert and how the hell am I supposed to rescue you if you do it yourself? You could give a lesser man a complex, you know that?"

"What do you mean, strand you in the desert?" She waved a hand toward the camel that had wandered several feet away. "You have a camel, don't you?"

"No thanks to you. I could have died of thirst waiting for you to wish yourself back to me. Maybe we need to find someone to change the rules. You obviously can't make a decent wish."

"Why you. I wish—"

Will kissed her long and hard. When she came up for air, her eyes were glazed. "What was I saying?"

With a gentle finger, he brushed her ebony hair from her face. "You were saying how sorry you were that you ditched me in the desert."

The dazed expression cleared and she took a deep breath as if she wanted to argue again. Instead, she stared at his clothing, her brows crinkling. "By the way, where'd you get those clothes?" She jerked her head toward the beast. "And where'd you get that?"

He fought the grin that threatened to take over his face. "Well, you see, there was this city in the middle of the desert. I borrowed the camel and the clothing from them."

Her eyes flooded. "You found it? You found Sand City?" She would have dropped to her knees if Will hadn't caught her in time.

"Yes, I did."

"And...my father?" she whispered, her fingers clutching at his robe. "Did you find my father?"

"Would he be about so high?" Will held a hand out even with the top of his head.

Kate nodded, tears trickling from the corners of her eyes.

"Does he have hair the color of his daughter's, with a little gray at the temples?"

"Yes!" She flung her arms around his neck and held him so tight he couldn't breathe. "He's alive. Oh God, he's alive." Then she shoved him away and looked up at him. "I want to see him."

"We have to get this camel back to Sand City. Do you want to ride back with me or wish yourself there?"

For a moment, she hesitated and then her face broke out in a sparkling smile. "I'll ride back with you."

Will's heart sang. She was willing to put her father off for an hour to be with him. "Come on. You can start an argument along the way if it makes you happy."

"I don't start arguments. You do!"

"Do not." Will smiled.

"If I waited around for you to rescue me I'd be dead."

"You really have a great way to stroke a guy's ego, you know that?" Will nudged the camel's knees and it dropped to the ground. "Get on."

"It's not my job to stroke your ego." Kate clambered up into the seat. "You're a big boy, you shouldn't need a woman to boost your confidence."

When Will climbed up behind her, he adjusted his robes to a comfortable position and settled into the seat. "Could you hush for a minute while I get this camel up and on its way? Sheesh, do you always have to have the last word?"

The camel lurched backward, planting its front feet in the dirt.

Taking advantage of the backward motion, Will circled Kate's waist and pulled her tight against him. And that was all it took. Her body against his ignited every cell.

As the camel pitched forward to get its back feet beneath him, Will again made the best of the wild movements to get even closer.

"Do you have to hug me so tightly?" she complained. "I can hold on by myself, you know? I'm not a child."

His hand rose up to the base of her sequined bra. "Oh, I know you're not a child." Turning the camel back toward Sand City, Will wondered how he could make it all the way back without exploding. With her backside resting against his front side, he couldn't help the instinctive reaction. His groin tightened, his cock pressing into her back. *Talk about something, anything.* "So what happened when you wished yourself out of the desert?"

She held herself ramrod straight, but the exaggerated sway of the camel's gait made her bump against his chest again and again, until Will finally tucked her against him. "It works better if we're moving the same direction. So what happened?"

"Nothing I couldn't handle," she said.

Her lofty tone didn't make Will feel any better. "Sheik Sayyid captured you, didn't he?"

She hesitated for a moment. "Yeah."

"He didn't hurt you, did he?"

"No," she replied, but a tremor shook through her.

Will's arm tightened around her waist. "How'd you get away?"

"That's the amazing thing." She half turned toward him, her blue eyes shining.

It was all Will could do not to kiss her.

"Qarim figured out I could wish my way out of things so he had me bound and gagged."

Will's fist tightened on the reins. He wanted to beat Qarim for treating Kate so badly.

"But the four guards they had on me didn't have a chance."

"Four guards? They must think you're pretty dangerous." He thought she was dangerous to his libido. How could he be so hot for her when they were riding on top of a smelly camel? But he was and the swaying motion wasn't helping. The more they swayed the more her ass rubbed against his cock. "So—" his voice squeaked and he cleared his throat. "How did you get away?"

"Like I said, those guards didn't have a chance. Haley, Moira and the girls came to my rescue."

"Did they take out the guards?" Will couldn't picture the brunette and the redhead having enough brute strength to take out Sayyid's burly guards.

"Oh yeah. They distracted them in a rather unusual way."

"How?"

"I'd rather not say." She shifted, her butt wiggling against the seat, scooting her backward into him.

Will's hand moved to her hip. "Careful."

"Why?" She twisted and stared down at the bulge in his robes. "Oh."

"What can I say? There's something about a girl in a harem outfit that I can't resist."

She turned around and kept her gaze forward muttering, "I know what you mean."

"What do you mean by that?" She wasn't telling him something and he wanted to know what had her so secretive.

"None of your business."

"Look, if we're going to share an hour-long ride you'd think we could get along."

"I like it when we argue." She purposely wiggled her ass against his cock, again. "It makes me hot."

Will's hand around her waist tightened and his heart jumped into his throat. "Hot? As in the temperature?"

"Yes."

The lump in his throat dropped to his belly. Damn.

"And no." She laid her hand over his resting on her belly and guided it downward until it was positioned above her sequined panty line.

"For godsakes, don't stop arguing now!" Will cried.

"Do I have to do everything for you? Now I see what they mean you can lead a horse to water but you can't make him—"

Will slipped his fingers beneath the scrap of fabric and tangled in the mound of hair over her mons. Sliding between her folds, he found her clitoris and launched a sensuous attack that left her gasping.

"Drink. Ohmigod." She leaned her head against his chest and rocked her hips forward to allow him better access to all of her.

His fingers traveled lower to dip into her warm creamy cunt. The camel's rocking motion shoved his fingers deeper. He added another and another until all four fingers pushed in and out of her pussy.

"Ummm." She rubbed her ass against his rock-hard erection. "Closer. I want you closer."

"Kinda hard to do on a camel."

She shot him a sly smile. "William Moreland, are you afraid of a challenge?"

"Not me." He jerked the camel to a halt, lifted her leg over the side to where she sat sidesaddle.

"What are you doing?" she squealed.

"Rising to the challenge." With a few quick tugs, he had the panty portion halfway down to her knees.

"Wait! These sequins are murder. Let me do that." She squirmed, almost fell twice and kneed him in the chin. Finally she ceased movement. "I wish these damned things were off, already!"

"I don't know why, but I get a bad feeling every time I hear those two words out of your mouth."

"Don't be so paranoid." Kate rolled her eyes. "If this wish works, it'll be in your favor!"

"And if it doesn't, I could be roasting in Hell again."

Thunder boomed and Will's stomach dropped to his knees, a natural reaction to having been sent on previous ride he didn't particularly enjoy.

"I only did that once. You can't keep ragging me about one little trip to Hell."

"Yes, I can. I like making you mad. The fringe benefits are fun." His hand splayed across her belly and slid into her sequined bottoms to find her wet pussy. "See? Mad can be fun."

The ground shook beneath them, making the albino camel sidestep so quickly Kate struggled to remain aloft, grabbing hold of Will's clothes.

When the animal settled, the sequined panties and sheer leggings were gone. Which left her bottom half bare. Then she swung one leg over the camel and sat facing Will with a cocky smile. "Well? Are you going to just sit there gawking, or are you going to show me what's under that robe?"

"Hold these?" He handed her the reins and lifted the front of his robes. The beauty of his present attire was that there wasn't anything under the robes, except one happy penis poking its head upward.

"Ah, now that's what I'm talking about. You might not be much of a knight in shining armor, but you do have a way with a sword." She reached out to take him.

But Will grabbed her hands before she got there. "What do you mean I'm not such a knight in shining armor?"

"Nothing. I didn't mean anything." Her gaze remained on his cock and her arms strained against his hold, reaching for her goal. "Good grief, Will, I'm hot and horny and you want to stop the train to argue?"

"Yeah. It's a matter of pride."

"My pussy is a leaking sieve and my breasts are aching for your touch, are you crazy? I'm practically in a lather, don't make me wait!"

He leaned into her face and said in a low sexy tone, "Pushy broad."

Her face flushed red. "I told you I don't like being called broad. It makes me mad."

"Good, because there's nothing like a mad broad to fuck like a whore." He slid his hands beneath her ass and lifted her up onto his thighs, balancing her above the business end of his penis. With one long finger, he tested her entrance. Oh yes, she was hot, wet and mad. Just the way he liked her. "Fuck me, whore."

Kate's eyes lit in a combination of what looked like anger and desire. She only hesitated for a moment before she grabbed his shoulders and leaned close to his ear. "How do you want it, sir? Hot and fast, or slow and easy? It's your dime."

"Give it to me hot and fast, broad." He reached behind her and unclasped her sequined strapless bra, releasing her breasts to dangle in his face. She had beautiful breasts.

"Can we get this camel moving?" Kate nibbled at his ear, her pussy sliding over him like a warm moist sheath. "I like the added motion. It makes me want to fuck that much more."

Will kicked as hard as he could and the camel lurched forward, making Kate sit down harder on him. She felt so good, all warm and wet.

As he lifted her up and down on his cock, she nipped at his earlobes and neck. "Do you want to know how Haley and Moira distracted the guards?"

Will barely heard her, he was so caught up in the erotic sensations of a slow-moving mount and a beautiful woman riding him. "Sure, tell me," he said, his voice sounding breathless to his own ears. All his blood was leaving his head and traveling south, engorging his cock. His balls tensed as he teetered on the edge of orgasm. No, not so soon. He wanted this moment to last all the way back to Sand City.

But Kate was determined to share her experience. She leaned close to his ear and told him in explicit detail all of Haley's and Moira's actions.

Halfway through her description, Will jerked the camel to a halt and came in an explosion of light, color and feeling, like a kaleidoscope shattering inside.

"You liked that?" she said, a satisfied smile lifting the corners of her lips.

"Couldn't you tell?"

She crossed her arms over her bare breasts. "And it's just like a man to come so soon when I haven't had mine yet."

"Just like you to deny a man his waning glory because of your selfishness, broad."

Her eyes narrowed. "Don't call me broad."

"How about whore?"

"Now you're talking. Do I have to show you again how it's done?" A slow smile curled her lips. "Another fuck-me lesson?"

"I think I can handle it this time." He grabbed her nipple between his teeth and chewed it softly until she moaned and leaned into his face. He let go of that one. "How's that so far?"

"You're showing signs of improvement."

He nudged the camel into a slow walk. Then his hand skimmed over her breasts and down her waist to her hips.

His cock was still inside her and he knew it would only take a little encouragement to get it up to full hardness again. But this was her show and he was determined to bring her to her knees with desire. He launched his assault on her clit, stroking a line from where they were joined upward, dragging creamy juices to lubricate his touch. He stroked, flicked and toyed with her.

Kate moaned, her head dropping back, her breasts pressing into his face. He buried his nose between the bouncing mounds and rubbed his cheeks against the inside. All the while he teased and touched her, until her legs tightened around his thighs and she gripped his shoulders her nails digging into his flesh. Then her body jerked and shook, spasming to the rhythm of his finger against her clit.

When she collapsed against him, she sighed. "That was incredible."

Will smiled. "I know. However, you should put some clothing on. Your father might not understand why you've arrived riding a man instead of a camel."

Chapter Ten

ΕΟ

Will and Kate rode into Sand City, saddle sore but satisfied. In a panic to find her panties, she had to stop and make herself think. Then she wished for a nicely tailored pair of slacks and a blouse, appropriate clothes for greeting the father she hadn't seen in over a year. And she'd given Will khaki pants, a polo shirt, an Indiana Jones hat and cowboy boots.

He tipped the hat a little to the side and smiled down at her. "Okay, so maybe your wishes aren't all bad."

The incredibly sexy way he smiled, combined with the dip of his hat, made Kate's heart flutter. How could she be so attracted to this man after only a couple days? It had to be lust. She turned toward their destination, afraid he'd witness more than she wanted him to observe in her eyes. "I can't believe it was there in front of me and I couldn't see it," Kate said, her breathing quickening as they approached the gate. A tall, dark-haired man wearing the white robes of an Arab stepped out. Was this one of the residents of Sand City coming to greet them? On closer inspection, she recognized the blue eyes and the ready smile.

"Daddy?"

He held out his arms. "Kate."

Will helped her slide off the camel and she ran into her father's arms. "Oh, Daddy." Her tears soaked her father's robes.

After a long talk with her father, a dinner feast and catching up on things at home, Kate looked around and wondered where Will went. When she'd begun her quest a year before, she thought all she wanted in the world was her father back. Now that he was free of Sand City, Kate didn't have a quest, a goal, something driving her. But she had a need as strong as her determination to find her father. A need for a man in her life to make her whole. Not any man. She needed one who wasn't afraid to stand up to her, who wouldn't be put off by her determination or argumentative ways.

Kate needed Will.

Had she made the ultimate folly and fallen for a hundred-and-six-year-old archeologist?

She found him standing in the garden outside his room, peering out over the desert.

"You left while I wasn't looking," she said softly.

"I needed some air." The sun hid below the horizon, the lingering glow fading into a million stars.

She hooked his arm with hers. "Want to find a camel?" Waggling her eyebrows she smiled up at him.

When he didn't smile back, a chill that had nothing to do with the cool desert night flittered across her skin.

He cupped her chin and stared down into her eyes. "I'm glad you and your father are back together."

Kate bit her bottom lip. Here it came. Will was leaving her. She knew it before he opened his mouth.

"Harry's not back." He glanced out across the dark desert. "I'm worried about him."

"And you're going to find him." It wasn't a question. She knew how Will worked. He cared about his friend and wouldn't stop until he knew the other man was okay.

Will nodded. "I have to. If I ever want to be free of the Stone of Azhi's magic, I have to go with him."

And when he freed himself of the stone's curse, he'd free himself of her. Kate's stomach knotted. "Is it so bad to grant my every wish?"

"Not really, only when you send me to Hell." He turned back to her and rested his hands on her upper arms. "And when you start arguments."

"I don't start them, you do." She resorted to anger to keep from crying. "Of all the egotistical things you could say—"

He leaned over and kissed her. "I know you love it too."

"Don't think you're getting the last word in." She stared up at him, trying to be angry and failing miserably when a fat, wet tear trickled from the corner of her eye.

"What's this?" He lifted a finger to catch the tear and raised it to his lips. "My Kate can cry?"

Another tear followed the first. "I'm not crying. It's the sand. I must have gotten sand in my eye."

"Liar." He kissed her forehead, then her leaky eye, his hands sliding around to pull her close.

Kate sniffed. "Am not." How could he be so nice when she was falling apart here? She leaned into his shirt and sniffed the purely male scent of Will. "Can't you stay?" Was that her begging a man to stay with her? Had Kate the conqueror gone weak?

"I can't," he said, kissing her forehead. "I have to finish this."

He didn't say anything about her coming with him. Did he intend to go alone? Kate couldn't ask the question, too afraid of his answer. So she bit her tongue in wretched silence, swallowing the urge to sob in his arms.

"Kate?"

Oh please, ask me to go with you. I'd leave my father to follow you. Please, ask me to go.

"Could you wish me to where Harry and Edie are?"

Her chest tightened and she pushed away from him, staring out at the night sky. Tears magnified the size and brightness of the stars and the gaping black hole where her heart used to be.

"I don't know what their situation is. It could be dangerous. That's the only reason I can guess they aren't already here." Will leaned against a column and tore at a leaf he'd plucked from a rosebush. "I think they need me."

I need you. There. She'd admitted it, if only to herself. She needed Will. But he didn't need her for other than a little swift transportation. "Sure. I'll get you there." And out of her life forever. With her father back, she could handle anything. Even a broken heart. "When do you want to go?"

He straightened. "The sooner the better."

"Fine!" She clapped her hands together. "I wish—"

With a quick step toward her, he pressed a finger against her lips. "Let me say something first."

Kate backed away from the warmth of Will's finger that sent tingling vibrations from her sensitive lips to every part of her body he'd touched so recently. Which would be every part of her body. "What's left to say?"

"I want you to know how much I've grown to care about you."

Lip service. Blood rushed into her head as anger mounted. Kate welcomed the humming behind her eardrums that numbed her hearing. Before he could get much further, she interrupted. "Save it. You have places to go, I have my father. The sex was good, let's not make it anything more than that."

"Can I get a word in edgewise, just once? I'll bet your father never told you to shut up when you were little. I'd even bet he never gave you a good spanking. Am I right?"

"My father would never raise a hand to me."

"Maybe he should have. Then perhaps you'd have a little more manners and let a man finish what he's saying, instead of interrupting and not letting him tell you what's on his mind."

"If I thought you had a mind, I wouldn't interrupt!" Her blood rushed through her veins and the more she shouted at Will, the hotter she got. So hot she wanted to strip naked and fuck him there in the garden under the starry desert sky.

"I wanted to say something nice and you made a big mess of it." He stepped closer and glared.

"If you'd get around to it, I wouldn't have to interrupt!" She bumped her breasts against his chest, the mere touch acting like an aphrodisiac. Could he just shut up and kiss her?

"That's it, I'm going to teach you the lesson your father should have taught you years ago."

"Oh yeah?" Kate struggled to think of a good retort when her brain was clouded with lusty thoughts of getting naked with Will. "You and whose army?"

"It only takes an army of one to win the war with you, Kate." He grabbed her and marched her to the nearest bench.

Excitement raced through Kate's system. Now they'd get naked and he would fuck her like her body screamed for him to do.

Will sat on the bench, yanked her arm until she lay on her stomach over his lap. Kate practically panted with anticipation. Boy, this was going to be good. Once the man made love to her again, he'd see that he couldn't leave without her. He'd beg her to stay.

Then Will's hand landed with a sharp smack against her backside.

"Ouch! That hurt!" she yelled. "I thought—"

His hand smacked against her rump again.

"What are you doing?" All thoughts of making love with Will flew from her head and her defenses kicked in gear. Kate struggled to sit up.

"I'm spanking you."

"What?" She sputtered then yelled when he slapped her again. "How dare you...you...man! If you're going to spank me, the least you could do is pull down my pants!"

His hand stopped in midair and he stared at her with a confused frown. When his face cleared, he broke into a grin and laughed out loud. "Kate Ralston, you are too much. Even when you're getting a spanking you make me laugh."

"I'm glad you're laughing, my ass is killing me," she groused from her position sprawled over his lap. "If you're done humiliating me, you can let me up and I'll wish you wherever you want to go, as long as it's out of here and away from me."

But Will didn't let her up. Instead, he reached beneath her, unsnapped her pants and slid the zipper down. "Not until you get what you deserve," he said, his voice husky.

The traitorous thrill shivered through her body again. How did her body do that when she was so angry? Maybe her sex drive was permanently connected to her anger drive.

No, she had been mad at Toad-the-Sleaze and had no sexual desire to fuck him. Now, Will, on the other hand—

The man on her mind and fanny slid her pants over her rump and down around her ankles. The cool night air caressed her bare bottom, followed shortly by Will's hand.

He skimmed over her naked ass and slapped the skin. It made a loud popping sound, but didn't hurt. Just enough of an impression to make her body juice up, lubricating in the expectation of more to come.

"Spank me, Will. I deserve it."

He smacked her ass again, this time he didn't raise his hand afterward. Instead, his fingers parted her cheeks and slid between, angling for the wet entrance to her pussy.

Kate's muscles tightened and she moaned.

"Like that?" He dipped his finger into her, drawing a liquid trail from her vagina to her anus. After circling the tight entrance with his moistened finger, he pushed into her.

Arching her back, Kate jerked upward. At the same time, Will slid his thumb into her cunt, swirling around the inner walls, tempting and teasing her. She gasped and tightened her channel around his thumb. "Don't you have somewhere you need to be?" she muttered, barely recognizing her raspy voice.

"Ummm. Yes, as a matter of fact, I do." His other hand reached beneath her blouse and bra, cupping her breast. With rough hands, he tugged at her nipple rolling the tip into a tight ball. "This the place you were talking about?"

"No, I mean, yes." With Will stroking her clit and breast at the same time, Kate couldn't think beyond those two points.

Then he stood, pulling her to her feet at the same time.

Was he done? Did he intend to leave? Kate's gut knotted and she struggled to stand with her pants around her ankles. Finally, she kicked free of the confining clothing.

"Having difficulties?" Will nibbled her earlobe, at the same time his fingers worked the buttons loose on her blouse. The back of his hand brushed against her breasts.

"You're taking too long." Pushing his hands aside, she quickly dispatched the remaining buttons and shrugged out of the shirt. As expediently, she unclasped her bra and tossed it onto a nearby rosebush. "That's how it's done."

Will stood back, his arms folded across his chest. "Just once, would you let me lead?"

She stood naked, her mouth open. "You have a nude woman standing in front of you and all you can do is talk?" She spun on her bare heel and marched away. "Find a wall to listen. I'm done."

Before she'd marched two steps, he caught her arm and yanked her back against him. "Did I say I didn't want you?" His hands pulled her hips back until her bottom rested against the hard ridge beneath his trousers. Oh, he wanted her, all right.

A victorious smile quirked the corners of her mouth and she wiggled her ass, rubbing the fabric of his pants. "I don't see you naked."

"If you'd give a guy a chance to perform a little foreplay, I might get naked. What do I have to do to make you realize a man's gotta have the upper hand in making love?" And his upper hand skillfully caressed her right breast.

"Okay," she said, with a little catch in her voice. "You can have the upper hand. Oh yeah, there. Right there. You can have the lower hand, too." She guided the hand at her hip around to the curls covering her mons. Twining her fingers with his, she dipped downward, parting her folds to find her ultra-sensitized clit he knew exactly how to please. Once she placed his hand there, he took over. "Now, you can lead." She sighed and leaned back against him, inhaling his musky scent.

With a finger he stroked a line up from her cunt, moistening her clit and swirling around it.

Her knees buckled and she clutched behind her for something to hold on to. With a gentle desert breeze caressing her skin, Kate teetered on the edge, clamping her legs around his hand as her body let loose, shattering into a thousand beautiful pieces, each spasm more intense than the last.

When she collapsed against him, he laughed softly in her ear. "Now, was it that hard to let me lead?"

She tensed, her competitive spirit rising to the challenge. "No, but now it's my turn."

Placing her hands over his, she slid them to her hips and then turned in his arms. Lacing her fingers at the back of his neck, she brought his mouth down to hers. Her tongue traced his bottom lip and pushed between his teeth where she stroked his tongue with hers. He tasted good, like mint and coffee. She could die like this, only she wanted more.

Deepening the kiss, her head grew dizzy from lack of air. She broke away and nibbled at his earlobe while she worked the hem of his polo shirt from his waistband. "How is it, I'm naked and you have yet to remove a single item of clothing?" She lifted the shirt up his torso and over his head, tossing it to the ground. His chest was gorgeous, tanned and sprinkled with light blond hairs. Kate laced her fingers through the hair, finding the dark brown nipples and teasing them to hardened nubs.

He grabbed her hands and held them away from his chest. "You're taking too long." Replacing her hands on his nipples, he unbuckled his belt, flicked the button free and unzipped his trousers, all within twenty seconds.

With raised brows, Kate stared down at his pants still riding his hips. "Pretty fast, but I don't see anything but boxers."

"That can be remedied." In one smooth motion, he had his pants and boxers off and he stood naked. Drenched in the light from a million stars, his skin glowed like a god.

Kate's breath caught in her throat. This was the first time she'd take the time to stop and stare at him. "Good God, Will, you're perfect."

"I know."

"Beast." She batted at his chest and he captured her hand.

"You bring it out in me, Kate."

"That's not all I'm going to bring out in you." She pushed against him, her power to seduce him a heady turn-on. "Sit. It's my turn to lead."

Will plunked down on the hard stone bench. "Ouch!"

"That'll teach you to spank me." With her knee she nudged his legs apart and stood between them. "Prepare to meet your match." Then she knelt on the hard ground and took his cock into her mouth. Swallowing him until he bumped against the back of her throat. She pulled back until the tip of her tongue balanced at the crown of his penis. A glance up showed her he wasn't immune.

His lips were pressed together and the muscle in his jaw twitched.

With her gaze on his face, she traced her tongue around the head of his cock, loving the taste of his velvety skin.

His hips rocked upward and his hand laced into her hair, pushing her down onto his cock.

She nipped at him.

"Hey!" He jerked back. "You could hurt a guy."

"I'm leading, here." She licked him from base to top, rolling his balls in her hands. "I'll have you begging me to suck your cock, before I'm done."

"Oh please, I'll beg you now. Please suck my cock."

"You're too easy." She slapped his thigh, stood and stepped back.

Will's eyes widened. "Where do you think you're going?"

"Not far. I want to try another tactic."

Then she climbed into his lap, sheathing his cock with her wet pussy. "There. Feel like fucking me like a whore?"

"Not really," he said, kissing her breast.

"What?" Was she not getting to him like he'd gotten to her?

"I want to make love to you, Kate. Like a man makes love to a beautiful woman." He pressed a kiss to her other breast.

His tenderness was her undoing. When he left, she wanted to remember him as a guy she slept with, not one who'd touched her heart. "I don't want you to. I want you to fuck me. Fuck me like a whore."

"I'm done playing games." He stood, taking her with him, still connected at that most intimate juncture.

With his cock hard and her legs wrapped around his waist, he walked her into the suite he'd been assigned.

"I don't want to make love to you in a bed," she said.

"Why? Afraid you might want more from me than sex?"

"Yes," she said in soft whimper. "I don't want to love you."

"Good, because I'm nothing but trouble." He laid her back against the sheets and bent over her, pulling a breast into his mouth and sucking hard.

"Exactly." Planting her feet on the side of the bed, she arched upward, taking him deeper inside.

"Make love to me, Kate. This might be all we have."

Anger warred with sorrow as she opened her legs and her heart to him, letting him in where no man had dared come before. Kate liked to keep men at arm's length to avoid falling for them and being disappointed. Only the shoe was now on the other foot. Some time between waking Will from the bottle and now, she'd lost. Lost her heart and her soul to this man she couldn't hang on to without her wishes.

"I could keep you here, you know," she said into his neck.

"But you won't." He moved his mouth to the other breast.

"No? What makes you so sure?" A tear slid down the side of her face and she hurried to brush it aside.

"Because you have a big heart beneath all the blustery bullshit you show everyone."

"I do not."

He kissed her lips in a feathery touch. "Do too."

They made love until the moon climbed to its zenith and fell from the sky into morning. When Will collapsed next to her, he draped an arm over his forehead. "I need to go. And you need to stay with your father."

No! Don't go. I love you so. Kate bit down hard on her tongue. "I suppose you do." And quickly, before she started crying in front of him.

He rose from the bed and walked out to the garden to retrieve his clothing. When he returned fully dressed he leaned over and kissed her. "Please, do it."

Kate pushed words past her frozen vocal cords, fighting back the onrush of tears. "I wish you were with Harry."

Chapter Eleven

ഇൗ

Will braced himself for the transfer and whatever he might encounter when he materialized. But he wasn't prepared to land in a supply closet with a naked Harry tied to shelf. "Harry! What happened? Yeesh, buddy, where are your clothes?"

"Untie me. I'll fill you in on the way." Harry jerked his head indicating the ropes holding his hands secure over his head. "What took you so long? I'd have thought you'd come looking for me a lot sooner?"

Heat rose in Will's cheeks. "I got tied up. Not like you, but busy, nonetheless."

"You got lucky, as they say nowadays, is what you're telling me." Harry shook his arms once the ropes were removed. "Kate?"

"Yes, of course."

"No of course about it. You had a reputation of being a love-'em-and-leave-'em man. Why should I think you were busy fucking Kate when you could have been saving my ass?"

"Don't get your hackles up with me." Will tossed the ropes to the side. "How was I to know your ass needed saving?"

Harry waved a hand in the air. "Did I come right back to the gates of Sand City like planned?"

"No, but then you and Edie could have been...well, you know."

His brows rose. "Do you see Edie anywhere?"

For the first time, Will registered her absence. "No. Where is she?"

Lips thinning, Harry's eyes narrowed into a fierce frown. "A woman named Danorah Hakala took her. She wants to trade Edie for the Stone of Azhi."

"Damn. You're not considering it, are you?"

"What else can I do?" Harry looked at him with a hard, angry look on his face. "She'll kill Edie if I don't give her what she wants."

"Harry, you've always been the sworn-to-the-death bachelor. Have you fallen for this woman, Edie? Does she mean that much to you?"

"My life." The unshakable Harry scrubbed his face with his hands, standing for a moment unmoving. Then he glanced back at Will. "She followed me here knowing how dangerous it was. She almost got herself killed trying to save me. She's perhaps the bravest and most adventurous woman I know."

"Yeah, she's pretty amazing," Will said. But he wasn't thinking of Edie, he was thinking of Kate. Hadn't she pursued the Eye of the Serpent relentlessly, marching head-on into danger, prepared to die to save her father? She was nothing like the women he'd dated in the past. Maybe that's why he couldn't shake her out of his system. As she'd shown him over and over, he'd met his match. The thought knocked him back a step or two.

"Are you just going to stand there like a lovesick fool, or are you going to help me find my clothes?" Harry clawed through the stacks of blankets, towels and cleaning supplies. "I have to get to the stone and to Edie before they do something stupid to her."

"Here, let me." Will joined his effort, tossing soap and shampoo to the side.

"Where's Kate?" Harry asked. "We could use her help too."

"She's not coming."

"Not coming? What do you mean, not coming?" Harry held up his shirt and shook the dust out of it. "No, wait. Don't tell me. You told her it was too dangerous and you didn't want her following you."

"Yeah, how'd you know?"

"It's the same bullshit I told Edie when I came looking for you." Harry headed for the door. "Let's just hope she really does love you and doesn't take as long to figure out you're a dope as Edie took to figure that out about me."

"Where are you going?"

"In case Kate isn't dumb enough not to fall for a louse like you, I have to get to that stone so that I have something to bargain with. I want Edie back."

"Where is it?" Will asked.

"In Iraq," Harry replied, yanking open the door.

"We're in Saudi Arabia. That's a country away!"

"I know. I have to hurry if I want to save Edie."

"Might be a good idea to wear pants." Will tossed a pair of slacks he'd found draped over the top of the shelf.

Harry slipped into his pants and shoes and stalked out of the hotel, hailing a taxi.

Will followed and threw himself in as the taxi pulled away from the curb. Of all the times to get noble and brush off a girl, he had to pick the worst. He needed

Kate's help right now. More than that, he missed her and he'd only been away from her for less than an hour.

"What are the chances of Kate following you here?" Harry asked, his gaze on the road ahead.

"I really don't know." That he didn't know Kate's mind made his chest feel empty and his heart disconnected. "We found her father and she's happy to be with him." Would she forget Will within a day?

Harry's gaze caught and held his. "Any possibility that she loves you?"

Sagging into his seat, Will turned away. "I don't know." Kate? Love him? After their constant arguments and him telling her not to bother following him? He doubted it. Now, not only did his chest feel empty, it felt tight and empty.

"God, I hope she does," Harry said.

"Me too," Will muttered and realized he meant it.

* * * * *

"I can't believe he's gone. Hell, I can't believe I wished him gone." Kate paced the floor in her father's room.

"I take it you care for him?"

"No — yes — oh, I don't know!" She flung her arms in the air. "He calls me a broad."

Her father's brows rose. "If I recall, you've decked men for calling you that."

"I know."

"You didn't deck him?" A smile lifted tipped the corners of his lips upward.

"No." She flung her hand out again. "I made love to him!"

"Huh?" He shook his head and laughed. "Maybe this is too much information for your father to hear."

"Dad, it doesn't make sense. I've known him all of a couple days, he drives me crazy arguing with me, but all I can think about is Will."

"You love him." Her father's words weren't a question. He was stating a fact.

"What?" Kate stared at her father as if he'd grown horns. "How could I love someone who contradicts everything I say?"

"Could it be because he's the first guy you've gone out with that has stood up to you?"

She fisted her hands on her hips. "He irritates me."

"And makes you complete?"

Her eyes filled and her arms dropped to her sides. "Yes."

"Katie, Katie. You know I love you." Her father pulled her into his arms for a brief hug.

"I know." It felt so good to be held in his arms after thinking he might be dead for the past year. But her father's arms were no longer enough. She wanted Will.

When her father set her at arm's length, he gave her a pointed look. "What are you waiting for?"

Kate shook her head and stared up into her father's blue eyes. "What do you mean?"

"How long do you think you need to know you're in love?"

"I don't know. A week or two. Maybe a month? How long did it take you and Mom to know?"

"I knew the moment I met her. It took me precisely two days to convince her she loved me."

"Really?"

He crossed a finger over his heart. "Honest."

"But I just got you back." Kate pressed her face into his chest. "How can I leave?"

"I'm safe and free. You can come visit me any time you like." He kissed her forehead. "So I say again, what are you waiting for?"

Hope dared to unfurl in her chest. "Are you telling me I should go after him? He told me not to."

"Since when have you done anything but what you wanted, Brat?"

She nibbled at her lip. Dare she? "I've always done what I wanted."

"So why stop now?" He circled his finger in the air. "Can't you do that wishing thing and get there faster?"

"Yes." She held on to her father's hands, her fear almost paralyzing her. "But what if he doesn't want me?"

"You won't know unless you ask." He embraced her again. "Now go before I change my mind."

"Okay." Butterflies rumbled in her gut as she anticipated her leap of faith. Would he be glad to see her or would he want her to go back home? She'd know soon enough. "Bye, Daddy. I'll be back as soon as I can."

"I love you, Kate."

"I love you, too." She shrugged and gave him a crooked smile. "Well, here goes." With her eyes squeezed shut, she made her choice. "I wish I were with Will."

Thunder ripped through the air and the floor shimmied. Kate opened her eyes and waved at her father as his face faded into blackness.

* * * * *

Will sat back in the cab, his thoughts not on the city of Riyadh passing by the window, but on a dark-haired, blue-eyed witch. What was Kate doing right now? Was she asleep in her bed? Naked? Will's body quickened, his pants uncomfortably tight.

"Are you going to do the honors, or am I?" Harry asked.

"Huh?" Will stared at his friend. "What honors?"

Harry inhaled and let his breath out as if preparing to explain things to a dull-witted idiot. "I don't have any money, do you?"

For the past couple days, Will had been on the run. Between dodging bad guys and a trip to Hell, money hadn't crossed his mind. "No."

"Other than this taxicab, we don't have any other way to get to Iraq, do we?"

"I can't think of one." The light came on. "Oh! You want to commandeer this cab to get us to Iraq, is that it?"

Harry smacked his palm to his forehead. "Why don't you say it little bit louder so our driver can get nervous?" He backhanded Will's arm and continued in a quiet voice only Will could hear. "Yes. We need this car to get to Iraq. Unless you have a stash of money to pay him, we'll have to take what we need."

"I say we get him to stop the car before we jump him." Will grinned. "It could get ugly if we knock him in the head while the car is in motion."

Breathing in then out, Harry stared straight ahead. "Tell you what. You stop him and I'll take care of the rest."

"What about identification and documents when we get to the border?"

Harry didn't have any idea what to do about border crossings, all he knew was he had to get to Iraq. "We'll worry about that when we get there."

"Then let's do it." Will leaned forward to tap the driver's shoulder. Before he could touch the man, Will was flung to the side, thunder booming in his ear. "What the—"

A body landed against his chest, knocking the air from his lungs. He raised his hands to block his face, squeezing his eyes shut.

"Hello, Will." A warm throaty voice whispered in his ear. A voice he couldn't forget. At first, he thought he'd been knocked unconscious and was dreaming of Kate.

Then feminine fingers pulled his hands away from his face. "Hey, you dope, it's me, Kate." Gone was the sexy tone, in its place Kate's normal challenging tone broke through.

Will opened his eyes to the woman who'd occupied his every thought since he'd left her back in Sand City. Now she sat on his lap crunching his balls in the backseat of a taxicab. Elation warred with anger. "What are you doing here?"

She grinned. "I came to see if you needed any help."

"No, we don't," Will replied automatically.

"Don't listen to him," Harry said. "Yes, we do."

She glanced from Harry to Will. "So, which is it? You do or you don't need my help?"

"Do," Harry said at the same time as Will said, "Don't."

What was wrong with him? Hadn't he been mooning over her for the past hour? Did he have a masochistic wish to hurt himself by pushing her away?

"I choose to respond to your friend," she said. "He seems to be the only one in his right mind at the moment."

"I know my mind, and I don't need you bailing me out at every turn." Will couldn't understand why his mouth didn't shut up when his heart was screaming at it to. Kate was here, right where he wanted her.

"Maybe I should switch laps?" Kate shifted her fanny.

Will's arms came up around her and that was all it took. The soft swell of her hips beneath his hands, her round bottom pressing against his straining cock, were his undoing. "Okay, so maybe we need your help, but just to get Edie back."

With a quick glance around the cramped interior of the cab, Kate asked. "Where's Edie?"

"She's being held hostage by a woman named Danorah Hakala," Harry said. "We need your help to free her."

"No problem. I'll help." Her brows rose and her mouth curved up on one side. "On one condition."

Uh-oh, Will didn't like that look or tone when she mentioned a condition. He braced himself.

"Anything," Harry said.

Speak for yourself, Harry, Will wanted to say, but kept his thoughts to himself.

"First, I want Will to admit he needs me." Kate crossed her arms over her chest and stared down her nose at Will.

"Will?" Harry jerked his head toward Kate.

Even in her regal, I'm-going-to-get-my-points-in-when-I-can way, Kate was sexy as hell and Will couldn't fight his desire. "Okay, I need you. But only to get Edie out of a jam."

Her brows wrinkled on her forehead and she paused for a moment before saying, "You need me for more than that, you're just too hardheaded to realize it."

"Am not. And quit being so pushy. Men don't like it when you order them around."

The color rose in her cheeks and Will knew he'd scored his own points. He added one more for the road. "I knew there was a reason I liked my women pliable."

Kate's nostrils flared. "No you don't."

"Yes, I do."

"Excuse me—" Harry said from the less volatile corner of the cab.

"If you did…" Kate continued, ignoring Harry's interruption. "You'd have married one by now and had a half-dozen air-headed children."

"That's just it, I don't want to get married and have kids. I like my life the way it is." Will could have kicked himself for sounding less than convincing, which made for an open invitation for Kate to pick him apart.

And Kate was up to the task of picking. "No you don't. You want a woman who's your equal and isn't afraid to tell you so."

"You think I want a pushy broad like you?"

Her eyes widened. "Did you just call me a broad?"

His lips lifted. "Yes, broad."

"Will?" Harry tapped on Will's shoulder, which Will promptly shrugged off. Harry appealed to the woman on Will's lap. "Kate?"

"You never stuck with a wimpy woman because they bored you within five minutes," she said. "Admit it."

Will pressed his lips together in an attempt to look angry. "No they didn't."

Kate crossed her arms over her chest and raised her brows.

"Ten minutes." Will admitted, a grin fighting for release. "But that's not the point."

Harry stuck his head in between Kate and Will. "Edie could be in danger, can you two stow it until we get her back?"

"I can, if he can." Kate's chin tilted upward.

Suppressing the overwhelming urge to kiss that pointed chin, Will said, "I can."

As she stared into Will's face, Kate's eyes narrowed. "We're not through."

"That's what you think," Will shot back.

"Enough!" Harry shouted.

The taxi driver swerved and pulled to the side of the road, glaring into his rearview mirror at the trio in the back and speaking in rapid-fire Farsi, his words much too fast and garbled for Harry to translate.

"It's okay, keep driving. We don't care where, just move." Harry gave the driver a weak smile and waved him forward. Then he glared at Kate and Will. "Can we get on with this?"

Will nodded. "Okay, okay, keep your shirt on. Kate, could you wish us to wherever Edie is?"

Before Will finished his request, Harry was shaking his head. "She can wish you and herself there, but she can't wish anyone else."

"Why?" Will asked.

"I don't know why," Harry replied. "But we found that when Edie tried to wish others to different places, it didn't work." He shrugged. "But it doesn't hurt to try."

Kate stared at Harry. "I wish Harry were with Edie."

Will tipped his head and strained to hear the sound of thunder.

Nothing. Over two minutes later, Harry still sat in the backseat of the cab.

"Guess you're right." Kate turned to Will. "That means it's up to the two of us. You game?"

"I suppose." He added quickly, "As long as you don't get mad and send me to Hell."

"Don't be so paranoid." She sat up straight in his lap and squinted her eyes. "Now, how to go about this."

"Danorah knows Edie can wish, so she had her gagged," Harry said. "She'll be expecting the unusual."

"Let's go." Will patted her backside.

"Just like a man to want to blow in guns ablazin' and no idea where and who to shoot." Kate shook her head. "No, perhaps I should go in as a fly on the wall and check it out first."

"No way." The thought of Kate going into danger without him had Will's gut turning flips. "I'm going with you."

"I wish I were a fly on the wall in the same room with Edie." Kate smiled at Will. "See you in a few."

"No, I won't let you. Anything could happen." With his hand planted on her hips, he held on, praying she wouldn't disappear.

"You're going to miss me, aren't you?" As the thunder boomed and the cab shook, she leaned close and pressed a kiss to his lips.

"Yes!" Will replied, but her image shimmered and she was gone. "Damn it!"

With a chuckle, Harry looked over at Will. "She'd have gone whether you wanted her to or not. That's one strong-willed woman you got there."

"Shut up, Harry." Will frowned at his former friend. "This is all your fault."

"What? That she chose to go ahead? I think Kate has a mind of her own and she's not afraid to use it."

"I know that. I mean this whole mess is your fault." Slumped against the back of the dingy taxicab, Will wanted to hit someone. "If you hadn't poked around in that smelly old tomb, we wouldn't be here."

Harry frowned. "And I would never have met Edie, and you wouldn't have known Kate."

Will sat in his corner of the cab glaring at Harry. "Exactly."

"Would you really rather go back to your life before Kate? As I recall, you had a girl or two in every port. And I bet you can't remember a single name."

Will closed his eyes and tried to picture the other women who'd faded in and out of his memories. None came into mind clearly and not a single name popped up. But Harry wasn't right, he couldn't be. "I liked my life."

"Did you?"

"Shut up, Harry," he said, without the anger of a moment before.

"You're worried about her, aren't you?" Harry stared out the window. "I'm worried about Edie."

Silence stretched as the taxi wandered around the streets of Riyadh, the meter clicking up a fortune in fares.

"What happened, Harry?" Will asked. "One moment, I'm a happily confirmed bachelor, the next I have this wild woman out of control in my life."

Harry gave him a knowing look. "You fell in love."

"I couldn't have." Could he? "She's all wrong for me."

"How so?"

"She's pushy," Will said.

His lips curling into a smile, Harry countered, "Or could it be she's strong?"

Will scrambled in his brain for everything wrong about Kate. "She's reckless."

"Adventurous," Harry shot back.

Oh yeah? Try, "Mouthy."

"Kate knows her mind."

She did know her mind, and Will liked that about her. Oh hell, what was the use? He sighed. "I love her."

"Yes, you do." Harry nodded.

"How could this happen?"

"It's like getting hit by a stray bullet on a two-million-acre ranch. Your chances of finding the woman for you are limited. But when that bullet pierces your heart, you're a goner."

Will's lips twisted and he shot an annoyed look at his friend. "I feel so relieved at the analogy. So, basically, I'm a dead man?"

Harry grinned and clapped him on the back. "That's right, Will. It's over. Your days of confirmed bachelordom are through."

"Then she better hurry back before I have to punch someone."

Once again, thunder boomed and the taxicab lurched.

Harry smiled. "Speak of the devil—"

"That's the truth and she has her own special way of sending you to Hell and back. I don't recommend it."

In the blink of the taxi meter, Kate appeared in his lap, the weight a welcome reminder she was back and in one piece.

"Whew! That was different." She placed a hand on either side of Will's cheek. "Do I look normal to you?"

"Definitely not."

"You're kidding, right? For once don't pull my chain. Do I look human?"

"Yes, you look very human." He ran his hands up her sides and back down to where her hips flared. "And if it helps, you feel human—all soft, feminine and curvy."

She swatted at his hand. "What I meant was do you see any traces of fly wings or antennae?"

Will ran his hands up her back and across her head. "No wings, no antennae."

She slumped against him. "Thank God. It worked so well going over, but I wasn't so sure coming back."

"You were actually a fly?" Will's eyes rounded.

"Yes, and it was perfect! I was there in the same room with Edie and with no one the wiser."

Harry grabbed her arm. "Is she okay? Where is she?"

"She's tied to a chair and gagged, but she looked okay. I had a chance to land on a window and saw a street sign." She leaned over the taxi driver's shoulder and gave him the name of the street corner. The driver frowned but took off, swerving in and out of traffic.

"There were two guards and a blonde woman there as well." Kate grinned at Will. "I think we can take them."

"What? Are you crazy?" He couldn't let Kate barge into a trap. She'd get herself killed.

"Here's my plan." Her eyes lit up and she leaned forward.

"Whoa, wait just a minute. You're not planning this event. You won't even be there."

"The hell I'm not!" she shouted. "It's my wish, I can do what I want."

"Hey, you two." Harry tapped on Will and Kate. "We're here."

The taxi driver pulled up to the curb and shifted into park.

Harry turned to Kate. "Anyone have money to pay the taxi?"

Kate glanced at Will and then to Harry. "Some date." She dug in her pocket and slapped Saudi Arabian *riyals* into the driver's hand. The man grabbed the money and jumped out to open the door for the trio.

"I have the feeling he wants us to get out," Kate said.

"And stay out," Will added.

Once the three stood on the sidewalk, Harry turned to Kate and asked, "What's your plan?"

"We'll give you five minutes to make it as close as you can. Then I'll wish Will and me into the room." She glanced from Harry to Will. "With me so far?"

Will's lips pressed together. "Did you leave any thinking for Harry and me?"

She frowned. "Are you trying to make me mad?"

He gave her his all-innocence smile and crossed his arms. "Maybe."

Harry clobbered Will in the gut with the back of his arm. "Edie's in there, be serious."

"I am." Will waggled his brows. "Okay, okay. Get moving, Harry. We'll see you inside."

Chapter Twelve

ഔ

After Harry headed into the building, four minutes and thirty seconds of silence stretched between Kate and Will.

The entire time, Kate kicked herself. *Say something, you idiot! Tell him you love him and don't want him to go without you.* She glanced at her watch. "You think he's pretty close by now?

Will grabbed her upper arms. "Kate?"

"Yes, Will?"

His mouth opened and closed, but nothing came out. Then he sighed. "I think it's time."

"Fine!" She shook off his hands. What had she expected, a declaration of undying love? From Will? "I wish—"

"No, wait." He reached for her hand and laced her fingers with his. "I just want you to know…"

Her heart screaming for him to finish his sentence, Kate couldn't wait any longer. "You love me, right?" She yanked his hand, pulling him up against her. "I know." Then she pressed her lips to his.

A long moment later, Will set her away from him. "That's just like you to put words in my mouth."

Kate rubbed her breasts against him. "That's not all I like putting in your mouth. Time's up. You can't take the words back."

"I never gave them, so how could I take them back?"

She flipped him a smile and leveled a steady, happy stare at him. "I wish Will were behind the guard by the door in the room with Edie, and I wish I was behind the guard behind Edie."

Thunder rang in Will's ears and his gut clenched. As the ground shifted beneath his feet, he reached out for Kate. "I love you, broa—"

With her heart near bursting, Kate's world went black and faded back into the color of white—the white robe of the guard standing behind Edie.

A little unsteady, Kate flung a side kick at the man's head, sending him staggering to his knees.

Will had the other guard by the throat, struggling to subdue him.

When the man Kate downed rose and turned to attack her, Edie stuck out a foot and the man toppled to his face with a loud thud. Kate had just enough time to kick him in the temple, rendering him unconscious.

Before she could congratulate herself, Kate noticed the struggle by the door wasn't going very well. The guard slammed Will backward against the wall, the sound loud enough to bring in reinforcements.

Kate cringed, feeling every bit of his pain. When she leaped across the room she was a second too late.

The door flung open and a blonde-haired woman rushed in with a pistol aimed at Edie. "Stop or I'll shoot her."

Halted in mid-stride, Kate stood still, darting a glance from Will to the blonde she assumed was Danorah. The hard glint of her brown eyes let Kate know the bitch wasn't fooling when she said she'd shoot.

Anger and frustration licked at her gut. Had they come this far in their fight to be stopped by one loaded gun?

As the thought surfaced, a man flung himself through the door, barreling into Danorah's back.

Kate threw a side kick at Danorah's hand and the gun went off.

Danorah crashed to the floor where Harry pinned her beneath him. "Grab the gun!" Harry yelled.

Kate dove for the pistol as another one of Danorah's thugs entered the room.

"Stop!" Rolling to her feet, Kate pointed the gun at Danorah's face. "Let's try it from this angle, shall we? Any one of your guys moves and I blow your pretty face away."

Hair askew and visibly shaken, Danorah cried out, "Back off."

The man slamming Will against the wall didn't have a chance. Will's persistence had finally paid off and the guy crumpled to the floor, blue-faced.

Will staggered away, shaking the arm he'd used to choke the air out of the big guy.

Kate's heart swelled. Her man had taken out the biggest bad guy. She wanted to run to him and tell him how proud she was. But she held the gun and all the cards in her hand.

In a quiet but steady voice, Will said to Danorah, "Tell your men to leave the room."

Danorah's lips pressed together.

Harry turned her face, forcing her to look him in the eye. "Tell them."

"Do as they say," she said.

After the men still standing left the small room, Will walked over to Kate and nodded at the weapon in her hand. "Want me to take that?"

"No, I have it under control."

"Yes, you do." Will glanced at Harry. "Let her up. I'll keep an eye on her."

Harry stood and hurried over to Edie, untying her bonds and removing the gag from her mouth. "Hey, sweetheart. Are you okay?"

"Yes, but she won't be when I'm through with her," Edie glared at Danorah. "Don't you ever give up?" she asked the woman.

Danorah dragged herself off the floor and stood, shoulders back and chin up. "I will have the Stone of Azhi. Nothing will stop me."

"Wanna bet?" Kate shot a smile at Will. "Hell isn't bad enough for a woman like her, is it, Will?"

He grinned back at her. "No, it's too nice a place."

"Since it's our only choice for now…" Kate jerked her head toward the redhead. "Edie, you want the pleasure or shall I?"

"Oh please," Edie's eyes narrowed, "I'd love to. Danorah, I wish you'd go to Hell." When the last word left her mouth, Edie clapped a hand over her lips. "I can't believe I did that. I've never done anything that mean."

"Feels good doesn't it?" Kate asked. "Especially, when they deserve it."

"No!" Danorah screamed.

But the thunder didn't vibrate the walls and Danorah still stood where she'd been a moment before.

Harry patted Edie's shoulder. "You can't wish others away. Remember?"

"What if we both wish together?" Kate asked.

"It's worth a try. On the count of three—"

"No! I'll leave you alone. I won't try to take the Stone of Azhi." Danorah dropped to her knees. "Please don't send me to Hell."

"You feeling sorry for her yet?" Kate asked.

"Not much." Edie rubbed her wrists. "But she does put on quite a performance."

"Wanna let her go?"

Edie's lips twisted. "It would be the right thing to do."

"Okay, blondie." Kate waved the pistol at her. "You can go, but you try anything, I'll use this. My daddy taught me to shoot so don't think I can't."

"I won't try anything. I promise." Danorah backed toward the door, yanked it open and dashed through.

"Remind me not to piss you two off." Will slipped an arm around Kate's waist and pulled her against him.

"That's right," Kate said. "You don't want to go back to—"

He kissed her hard. "I don't even want to hear that word from you ever again. Damned pushy broad."

"Are you trying to pick a fight with me?" She kissed him back.

"You bet." His hands slid up her back inside her blouse.

"What say we get the hel—heck out of here?" Harry stood behind Edie, his arms firmly wrapped around her.

"I'm all for it." Edie glanced up behind her. "Where to?"

"We could use a little rest and relaxation before we go on to find Mitch." Harry waggled his brows and then his face grew serious. "I missed you."

"I missed you, too." Edie turned in Harry's arms and laced her hands behind his neck.

"I didn't get much time with my father." Kate glanced at Will. "Could we make it Sand City?"

"Are you asking my preference?" Will looked over her shoulder. "Where did my Kate go—the one who makes her own decisions and mine too?"

Kate's heart sang. He'd said "my Kate" like he might want to keep her around, but she couldn't resist sparring. "Look, don't make me regret asking."

Harry shook his head. "These two could be at it for a long time and I don't plan on waiting until Danorah and her goons come back in." He smiled down at Edie. "Sand City?"

She nodded. "I wish we were in Sand City."

"See that?" Kate said as Edie and Harry disappeared before their eyes amidst the crash of thunder and a little earth shaking. "While you were flapping your gums, they left."

"So what are you going to do about it?"

"I wish we were in that really gorgeous garden in Sand City." Once she had her wish made, she crossed her arms over her chest. "If we're going to be in any kind of relationship we need to get some things straight first."

"Are you going to go get pushy on me again? Some broads go a bit too far. And this broad," he pulled her into his arms, "goes even farther. Are you as hot as I am?"

Thunder rumbled around them and the floor trembled.

She nodded. "Hotter. Think we could get naked before the transfer?" Kate had her shirt up and over her head and Will had his pants down to his knees when the world began to fade to black.

Kate laughed. "Guess that answers—"

The End

Enjoy an excerpt from:
GHOST WIND

ಐ

Cleanly kept, the pioneer cemetery was surrounded by a wire mesh fence, and from the looks of the two gates across the semicircular pathway leading into and out of it, the little country burial ground most likely was locked after dark.

Lannie got out of the car, pulling on her car coat for there was a stiffening breeze blowing from the open field across the gravel road from the cemetery. Clouds were building to the southwest and there was a hint of moisture in the air. Snuggling the coat's collar up against her neck, she began walking through the gravestones.

For over an hour she surveyed the markers then looked off to the east where rolling hills dipped lazily behind the wire fence. The trees were spectacular in their fall foliage and she strolled over to the fence to get a better look at the valley beyond and a farm house sitting far off to the north of the hills. She was about to turn away when she noticed two gravestones that lay outside the perimeter of the fence, on the property upon which sat the deserted house.

Barely viewable through the thick bushes growing up around them, it was the stark white of the slabs against the weeds that had drawn her attention. Over the markers grew a large white oak tree with spreading branches — some of which dragged against the slabs, scraping across the surface like skeletal fingers.

She walked over to that side of the fence to see if she could read the markers but was surprised to find the slabs bare of any lettering. Why, she wondered, would someone go to the trouble of providing a burial slab but leave it unmarked? And why would the two graves be outside the borders of the cemetery proper on what must be private property?

Curiosity got the best of her and she scaled the fence—ripping a hole in the leg of her jeans.

"Shit," she said, looking down at the tear in her clothing. Sighing heavily, for the jeans were practically new, she dusted off the rent in the material and shook her head. "That's what you get for trespassing, Lanelle," she chastised herself.

Hoping nothing deadly was slithering along the ragged prairie grass surrounding the graves, she went to stand over them. Around her, the wind moaned through the black walnut trees and set the few remaining leaves on the arching branches to rustling.

There was no indication at all of who could be buried in that place so she turned to look at the side of the farmhouse. From that angle she could see the wraparound porch ended in a screened room that faced what had to be a gorgeous view of the little valley beyond with its vibrantly colored ashes, maples and beech trees. Once more she looked out across the road to the west side of Jewel Street, admiring the wide-open space and the privacy the farmhouse had.

It was then she noticed the For Sale sign half hidden amidst the rambling bushes that had overtaken the front yard of the farmhouse. Handwritten in red letters on a weathered white board, the sign looked as though the ravages of the harsh Midwestern weather had half torn it down over time. It wobbled back and forth as the wind pushed against it and, as she watched, finally fell to the ground to be buried among the underbrush.

For the longest time she stared at the place where the sign had fallen. Brought up to believe nothing ever happened without a reason, she had the strongest notion she had been meant to find this house out in the middle of nowhere. As though it had been an omen, she had been shown the For Sale sign only moments before it disappeared into the underbrush. Chewing on her lip, she looked about the property and knew she would find peace here. She knew she could do her writing without interruption and that appealed to her. But not as much as thinking perhaps her ex would have a hard time finding her in the boondocks of Iowa.

Nodding at her thoughts, she turned to retrace her trip over the fence but the glint of metal made her snap her head around. The sun had taken that moment to pop out from behind the scudding clouds overhead and had shone its light on something hanging from one of the oak's branches. Carefully making her way through the dense clusters of weeds encroaching on the grave slabs, she looked up at a medallion dangling from a golden chain.

Swinging in the breeze, the chain was snagged on a twig, the medallion twisting and turning back and forth. By jumping up a few times, she was able to reach the chain and pull it off, thankful the chain didn't break in the process. With the necklace clutched in her palm, she stumbled against the tree as the first drops of rain began falling. Looking across the road, she saw the clouds had darkened considerably and now flashes of lightning could be seen.

Stuffing the necklace into the pocket of her jeans, she climbed carefully back over the fence, making sure she did not do more damage to her clothing. She had to sprint to her car for the rain started in earnest.

As the rain slashed brutally down on the windshield of her borrowed car, Lannie fished in her pocket for the medal. Opening her palm, she saw three initials on the back of the medallion—R.B.D.—engraved into the gold in block letters. Turning the medallion over, she found it was a Saint George medal with the saint sitting astride his mount as he slew the dragon with a broadsword.

Tracing the design with her index finger, she felt a chill spread up her arm and shivered. A ferocious boom of thunder shook the ground beneath the car and she turned fearful eyes to the storm. Hanging the medallion attached to its gold chain over the rearview mirror, she cranked the car and drove slowly out of the cemetery, retracing her trip out to Highway 6.

He watched her driving out of the cemetery, his amber gaze locked on her car as it turned the corner onto North 39th Avenue East and disappeared over the hill.

He slowly closed his eyes.

For a long time he stood there with his eyes shut, his mind centered on the fleeting glimpse he'd had of her face. It was a face he longed to touch. He wanted to place his lips against the soft-looking flesh of her lips and taste the sweetness he knew lurked there. He wanted to hold her in his arms, press her cheek to his chest and hear her soft breathing as he stroked her back. He ached for something he had not known for many years.

Opening his eyes, he stared out over the rain-swept cemetery and the one grave that had drawn him to it every day for the last sixteen years. He had lost track of the times he had knelt before that black marble slab, spoken softly to the one lying beneath the soil.

Pain lanced through his chest and he hung his head, a single tear slowly falling down his cold cheek.

Memories could be evil and his were destroying his immortal soul.

Why an electronic book?

We live in the Information Age — an exciting time in the history of human civilization, in which technology rules supreme and continues to progress in leaps and bounds every minute of every day. For a multitude of reasons, more and more avid literary fans are opting to purchase e-books instead of paper books. The question from those not yet initiated into the world of electronic reading is simply: *Why?*

1. *Price.* An electronic title at Ellora's Cave Publishing and Cerridwen Press runs anywhere from 40% to 75% less than the cover price of the exact same title in paperback format. Why? Basic mathematics and cost. It is less expensive to publish an e-book (no paper and printing, no warehousing and shipping) than it is to publish a paperback, so the savings are passed along to the consumer.

2. *Space.* Running out of room in your house for your books? That is one worry you will never have with electronic books. For a low one-time cost, you can purchase a handheld device specifically designed for e-reading. Many e-readers have large, convenient screens for viewing. Better yet, hundreds of titles can be stored within your new library — on a single microchip. There are a variety of e-readers from different manufacturers. You can also read e-books on your PC or laptop computer. (Please note that Ellora's Cave does not endorse any specific brands.

You can check our websites at www.ellorascave.com or www.cerridwenpress.com for information we make available to new consumers.)

3. *Mobility.* Because your new e-library consists of only a microchip within a small, easily transportable e-reader, your entire cache of books can be taken with you wherever you go.

4. ***Personal Viewing Preferences.*** Are the words you are currently reading too small? Too large? Too… ANNOYING? Paperback books cannot be modified according to personal preferences, but e-books can.

5. ***Instant Gratification.*** Is it the middle of the night and all the bookstores near you are closed? Are you tired of waiting days, sometimes weeks, for bookstores to ship the novels you bought? Ellora's Cave Publishing sells instantaneous downloads twenty-four hours a day, seven days a week, every day of the year. Our webstore is never closed. Our e-book delivery system is 100% automated, meaning your order is filled as soon as you pay for it.

Those are a few of the top reasons why electronic books are replacing paperbacks for many avid readers.

As always, Ellora's Cave and Cerridwen Press welcome your questions and comments. We invite you to email us at Comments@ellorascave.com or write to us directly at Ellora's Cave Publishing Inc., 1056 Home Avenue, Akron, OH 44310-3502.